"Relax, sweetheart," Leo urged

"Am I so easy to read?" Brenda whispered, gazing up at him, her heart racing.

"Yes," he whispered back, as if afraid to break the mood. His fingers moved tantalizingly across her back. "I can see that you're frightened of me, but at the same time, I think I see a spark of desire in your big brown eyes."

"You think?" A warmth suffused her, one that she hadn't experienced in years.

"I hope." Tentatively he nuzzled the sensitive skin at her neck.

With a deep sigh, Brenda relaxed. "Oh, Leo," she murmured, pulling him closer, reveling in the feel of his aroused body. There was no turning back now. . . .

With *Something to Treasure*, the story of
Leo and Brenda, **Rita Clay Estrada** wraps
up her delightful trilogy. Both characters,
you might recall, appeared briefly in the
previous two books, *A Woman's Choice*
and *The Will and the Way*.

Rita tells us that, like Brenda, she was once
an avid coupon clipper. In fact, with the
money she received on rebates, she
financed a trip to Disneyland! This
resourceful author lives in Texas with her
husband, James, and their four children.

Books by Rita Clay Estrada

HARLEQUIN TEMPTATION
48—THE WILL AND THE WAY
72—A WOMAN'S CHOICE

These books may be available at your local bookseller.

Don't miss any of our special offers. Write to us at the
following address for information on our newest releases.

Harlequin Reader Service
901 Fuhrmann Blvd., P.O. Box 1397, Buffalo, NY 14240
Canadian address: P.O. Box 2800, Postal Station A,
5170 Yonge St., Willowdale, Ont. M2N 6J3

Something to Treasure

RITA CLAY ESTRADA

Harlequin Books

TORONTO • NEW YORK • LONDON
AMSTERDAM • PARIS • SYDNEY • HAMBURG
STOCKHOLM • ATHENS • TOKYO • MILAN

This book is dedicated to four fantastic friends
who know the true meaning of the word:
Joan Hohl, Gayle Link, Kathie Seidick and
Patsy Rutkauskas. Thank goodness we met!

Published March 1986

ISBN 0-373-25200-5

1

SHE WAS LATE AGAIN. Brenda hurried down the red carpeted aisle, her dark skirt swaying gently with her steps.
Everywhere she went she was late! And she had so
looked forward to standing in the lobby and sipping a
glass of champagne, smiling charmingly at strangers as
if she really belonged here. It was an important part of
the whole experience of coming to a new musical and
something she rarely got to do. Brenda cursed herself
thoroughly for her faults as she spied her seat and began the crablike trek between the seats and other pa-
trons' knees.

The musicians tuned their instruments, each blend-
ing into a cacophony of sound. Voices murmured
throughout the theater as the lights dimmed. The show,
Carmel Clowns, was about to begin.

Finally, with flashes of smiles and apologies for stepping on others' toes, Brenda found her seat and grate-
fully plopped into it. She turned her body slightly so
that she could quickly tuck her brown purse out of the
way, only she received an elbow in her ribs for her
trouble.

"Sorry," the man next to her murmured, not even
looking in her direction. He was huge. He was also
gorgeous, with blond hair and bright eyes that stared

toward the orchestra pit to show off a perfectly straight nose. She followed the direction of his gaze, immediately finding the object of his attention. His eyes were focused on the lush redhead who held the cello so gracefully between her legs.

Brenda grimaced. Men! They were all the same; if there was a woman in their sphere with bright-colored hair and big eyes, then they fell for the romance of the moment. But let the reality and problems of day-to-day living intrude, and they ran like little boys hiding from chores.

She glanced sideways again, wondering if she could ask the man to move his elbow and allow her to have one of the armrests. Both men, the large one on her left and the much older gentlemen on her right, were using them. Anger built inside her. Wasn't that just like a man? They were never sensitive enough to realize that others might need their own space, too.

Slowly the gold curtain rustled, then began its ascent into the ceiling. Three spotlights aimed toward the shadows. One person began to sing, with the others joining in, one at a time. It was very effective, Brenda thought, since she continued to stare at the shadows to see the faces. The musical had begun.

Without consciously realizing what she was doing, she placed her elbow at the back of the armrest on the left of her. Slowly, very slowly, she pressed the large man's arm up farther so that she could rest hers without being cramped. The voices rose in striking harmony, giving her goose bumps of pleasure. The melody completed, the lights died, leaving only one spotlight at center stage, and she leaned back with a contented sigh.

"If you want my armrest, all you had to do was ask," the man on her left whispered in a deep, gravelly voice as he inclined his head toward her.

"Since it wasn't your armrest, I didn't see the need," she answered shortly. "You have another to your left."

Golden-brown brows rose pointedly, hazel-green eyes snaring her brown ones. "If that's the case, then you must have one to your right. Ingenious, the way they made two of them for each seat, isn't it?" His bland look told her more than words could. The man was laughing at her! Irritation quickly turned to anger.

She clenched her teeth to keep from shouting at him. "Perhaps you'd rather find another seat?" she gritted sweetly, which was hard to do. "A man your size must need—" her eyes flitted down his large body "—lots of room."

His big hand rested on the dark blue fabric that covered his tree-trunk thigh. The long strong fingers curled at her words. She smiled. Let him take that any way he wanted to.

The singing of one lone clown in the spotlight filled the air, and once more Brenda ignored the man next to her, lost in the notes of the music. Her complete attention was on the stage until intermission.

When the curtain came down and the lights went on, she blinked, returning from her fantasyland to her seat. She sighed, then stood, following the elderly couple in front of her as they marched up the aisle and into the lobby. She walked directly to the bar, ordered a glass of champagne, then found the perfect spot on the wall from which she could people-watch unobtrusively.

It felt so good to be out with adults for a little while. She almost, but not quite, felt guilty about the three small children at home who had wanted to come with her. But there had been no way to arrange it, thank goodness. Her boss, Sam Lewis, had given her his ticket and told her to go out and enjoy herself. He knew how badly she needed to feel just part of a crowd occasionally, instead of constantly juggling, sometimes fumbling, with the hats of secretary, mother, breadwinner and all the other things she did that gave no credit to a single parent.

Dear, sweet Sam had instinctively known, though. He realized that she needed an occasional break to be nobody, have no demands, and just blank out to everything but the enjoyment he always seemed to provide in the form of theater tickets, sports and premier-movie passes, and sometimes even a symphony or opera ticket. At least once every two or three months he was begging her to take his tickets and use them since he, and now his new bride, Catherine, couldn't go for one reason or another.

Tickets. A bell went off in her head. He had usually given her two tickets and told her to take a date with her, which she did: another secretary or one of the children. But this time he had only given her one ticket.

She frowned. Did that mean he had bought the ticket for her on purpose? Or had he given the other ticket to someone else? Like the huge bear of a man sitting next to her? It would have to be him because the elderly man on her right was with his wife, and Sam never had three tickets.

With a heavy sinking feeling in the pit of her stomach, she knew without confirmation that she was right. Her boss *had* given the man on her left his other ticket. He was probably a client or business associate of Sam's, and she had been insulting him for the past forty-five minutes in both word and look.

Her eyes searched the crowd, only to stop when she found the giant standing at the bar in an obviously tailored, three-piece, dark blue suit. His blond head was tilted, his green eyes twinkling with humor as he stared down at the svelte woman dressed in black next to him. The woman was obviously flirting, batting her lashes and allowing her pearly white, orthodontic-perfect teeth to show through carmine lips. Brenda's eyes never wavered as she watched them, filing through the friends and acquaintances that she knew Sam knew. Nothing registered.

Without seeming to, she began meandering toward the bar area, her eyes flitting here and there as if she was just wandering around the room with no purpose in mind.

Eventually she reached the bar. Now what? Should she interrupt the duet and ask the giant his name? Should she wait until they returned to their seats and then apologize for being so rude about the armrest? That stuck in her throat. No matter who he was, he shouldn't have monopolized those armrests! Just because he was a man didn't give him any more privileges than she had. It was the principle involved!

After ordering and receiving another glass of champagne, Brenda moved closer to the back of the woman in the black dress. The woman gave a throaty chuckle, brushing the hair back from the side of her face in a sensuous gesture. "Leo, you haven't changed a bit since the last time I saw you," she said, as if delighted with the fact.

"Neither have you, Irene. Still beautiful and elusive, traveling constantly from one continent to another, I hear." Brenda hated to admit that he had a deep bear-growl of a voice that was very melodic and soothing.

Leo? Leo who? She ran back over her mental list of Sam's clients and came up blank. Yet the name sounded familiar.

"Are you defending Regina Henderson?" the woman named Irene asked. "Rumor is that she's going for a multimillion dollar settlement." The silence was electric as Brenda waited for his answer. If she remembered correctly, Regina Henderson, a striking redhead, had married a millionaire and now, six years later, was claiming mismanagement of her personal funds.

Her mind buzzed with thoughts, one tumbling over the other. Redhead. Redhead. Of course! The bear of a man was Leo Coulter, her boss's best friend and known to be personally involved with every beautiful, long-legged redhead in the state of California! He was the proverbial love'em-and-leave'em type! Bile rose in her throat, and there was a buzzing in her ears that blocked out everything but her own anger.

Exactly the kind of man she hated. No, hated wasn't a strong enough word. Despised. Yes, and loathed. The plastic champagne glass in her hand cracked and she stared down at it, surprised to see her knuckles were white and her fingers tightened around the slim stem.

The lights blinked off and on, signaling everyone to take their seats. Brenda placed the still-filled glass on the counter and, with wooden steps, walked toward the double doors that led to her seating area.

Leo Coulter. He was the embodiment of everything she disliked. Good-looking, egotistical, arrogant, and firmly believing that redheads were supposed to be supplied to him every night of the year, then discarded when he tired of them. The only redeeming quality he had was that her boss held him in high esteem. And although Sam was a one-in-a-million-type man, he was also not infallible. Leo Coulter must be his weak spot.

She sat down, staring straight ahead over the orchestra pit and toward the gold curtain. She would ignore him. But first, she would take the armrest that rightfully belonged to her! Placing both her elbows on either side of the rests, she waited.

She was spoiling for a fight and she knew it. But she couldn't seem to control her thoughts or actions right now. She wasn't even sure she wanted to. She had to maintain control in every other facet of her life that an imaginary confrontation with *that man* would be welcome!

As if she conjured him up, he appeared at her knees. "Excuse me," he murmured politely, but she could tell he hadn't really even seen her.

"If you insist," she said under her breath, barely moving her legs to give him enough room to squeeze through to his seat.

He sat down and gave a sigh. His broad shoulders were even broader than she had thought, and without the armrests to give him the spread he needed, he looked as if he were a bear squeezed into a fox's den— all scrunched uncomfortably together. She repressed the giggle that formed. Besting him out of his armrest was enough; she didn't have to chuckle to let him know she had outmaneuvered him.

The lights dimmed and the musical began once more. Within minutes Brenda was lost in the story and lyrics, loving the lilting tunes that she knew would haunt her for weeks. Perhaps she could find a radio station that played them and record them for her cassette, for there was no way she could afford to buy the cast recording.

When the curtain fell and the audience began clapping, she blinked, tumbling once more back into reality. The cast received three curtain calls before the houselights were turned on and people began to file out.

Brenda sat watching the musicians fold and store their music sheets. Totally relaxed for the first time in weeks, she played one of the mellower tunes over and over in her mind.

"Pardon me, but are you ready to leave yet?" Leo turned in his seat as if to stand, pretending he was patiently waiting for her to move first.

The tune was lost, disappearing as Leo Coulter's face leaned toward her. "No, I'm not. I'm not stupid enough or in that much of a hurry that I want to get crushed in the mad dash up the aisle." She gave a fake smile that she was sure he could read correctly. "But if you want to join the throng, please, be my guest."

He leaned back, his eyes appraising her. His brow furrowed. "Have I done something to offend you, ma'am?"

"Of course not. I don't even know you," she snapped, irritated that he should be so direct. She wouldn't admit to the feelings his "ma'am" gave her. He probably wouldn't talk to the cello player that way!

"Then what is the matter that you can't seem to be civil to me?"

"You flatter yourself. I don't care a snap about you, one way or the other." Brenda was vastly annoyed.

"I don't give a snap about you, either, but that doesn't give me license to be purposely rude to you. Is it just me, or is it all men?" he persisted, his low gravelly voice irritating her. How many women had heard that dark, polished voice and were seduced by it? Well, not her, she knew better. Leo Coulter was the epitome of the California playboy.

She smiled sweetly. "Since I seemed to get along just fine with the gentlemen on my right, it must be you."

His green eyes narrowed. "Since the other gentlemen must be an octogenarian, he doesn't count. So I'm asking again . . . just what is it I'm supposed to have done? Besides hogging my armrest for the first part of the musical," he added caustically.

"You wouldn't understand," she muttered.

"Probably not," he retorted, telling her exactly what he thought of her "understanding." "But I still can't see you acting like a persimmon in full bloom over such a small incident."

The truth of his words hit home. Brenda started. He was right. What had he done? Had her attitude turned so bitter that others—those who didn't even know her—could see her as a persimmon?

"Never mind," she mumbled. For the first time since she had sat down next to him, she was embarrassed at her own behavior. The lift the music had earlier given her disappeared suddenly. She was back to reality with a bang all right. She was the bitter divorcée struggling to raise three kids on a salary meant for one. She was over-the-hill, overweight, brown haired, brown eyed and browned off. Anyone, man or woman, would call her "ma'am." *Especially* a lady-killer. She was thankful that he didn't know who she was.

"The crowd has thinned," she said, standing, then reaching for the brown purse she had tried to hide by her side earlier. It was small, but it certainly didn't match her black patent pumps. "Goodbye, Mr. Coulter." As she straightened up again, his eyes caught hers. He slowly rose, practically towering over her.

"Hurray for the crowd." He smiled mockingly, then gave a small bow as his hand ushered her toward the main aisle. "After you, ma'am."

Ma'am. There was that hateful word again, used as if she were on the downslide of life . . . at thirty-three. With her eyes sparking anger and her chin lifted determinedly, she stalked up the aisle, her small purse swinging in her hand in rhythm to her steps.

Without looking back, she crossed the lobby and went out to the large underground parking lot, her heels clicking with resolve, aiming like a homing pigeon toward her small, once-golden Volvo. She knew he wasn't far behind her. She could hear his muffled footsteps and they made her want to run and jump in the driver's seat,

locking the door behind her. Panic fluttered in her
stomach but reason won out. With every ounce of
stubbornness she possessed, she forced herself to continue the same pace as before. When she reached her
car, she glanced in his direction.

He wasn't there.

Fumbling with her key, she finally opened the door
and slid across the faded slipcover of the driver's seat.
She pulled the door closed, pushed the lock down and
held on to the steering wheel. Her hands were shaking,
her stomach queasy, her eyes were burning as if she
wanted to cry.

It took several minutes of deep breaths before she felt
calm enough to start the car and pull out of the parking
slot and up the ramp that would take her into the line
of traffic, and home.

Her thoughts bumped chaotically against each other,
none of them making sense except one.

There was no excuse for her rudeness tonight except
that it was a habit born of the past three years; it was
her own personal form of survival. For the first time
since David had left her, she had seen herself through
someone else's eyes, and she wasn't too thrilled with the
picture. It was time to take stock of herself and see what
she was becoming and where she wanted to go in life.

LEO FOLLOWED the brunette up the aisle, his irritation
at her behavior finally dissipating. He was usually an
easygoing man, but tonight he had allowed his control
to slip—just a little—and he didn't like it. What on earth
had he done to provoke her, and why did it bother him
one way or the other?

And she knew his name. Did that mean that she knew him or knew *of* him? And where did she know him from? He wasn't about to ask and hear that sharp tongue again. He didn't care that much.

He watched the swing of her hips, the jaunty, tight-bottomed walk and his hand would have loved to have reached out and touched just one side of her lovely jiggle. His hand clenched. Was he crazy?

He grinned. No, but she was. She had hang-ups on top of hang-ups, if he was any judge. Besides, she wasn't even a redhead. And her legs, although seemingly shapely through her black skirt, were not long and lithe, but soft and fully rounded. Not fat, though, just . . . pliant.

Her eyes were pretty, her mouth full and slightly pouty, her lightly freckled face a diamond shape that was intriguing. Her manners, boorish.

Leo shook his head from side to side in wonder as he watched her walk just slightly ahead of him. She was a case! How in the hell did she get ahold of Sam's other ticket? Sam had to have given it to her, but she didn't seem to be his type. She wasn't one of his sisters, nor was she part of Sam's office staff that he had met. It had to be someone he knew personally, but from where? Leo knew better than to think Sam might be fooling around with Miss Bitter. Especially now, with him staying so close to home as his and Catherine's first baby was due within the next few weeks. Sam, the eternal playboy, had gotten caught by one of the country's most talented and wealthiest singers, and so far, he hadn't regretted a moment of it. In fact, he was becoming boring on the subject of matrimony, thinking everyone should be tied so.

Oh, well . . .

Leo stood by his car, a midnight-gray Cadillac, as he watched the woman in the black skirt, black heels and brown purse, unlock her car and slip into the seat. He was three aisles away, just close enough to ensure that she was safe. Good, she was locked in.

He followed suit, stretching his substantial frame comfortably in the large interior. His hand was turning the key when another car pulled out, leaving him with a view of the used-to-be-gold Volvo. Now it was a dull, drab yellow. She was still sitting there, her head resting on the steering wheel. He frowned.

Dammit! What was the matter with her? Better still, what was the matter with him that he should worry about her? She had been rude to him from the very beginning. When he had finally called her a persimmon, though, he had seen the shock and hurt in her eyes, which was really absurd considering the other names he could have called her—and justifiably so.

Impatient with himself, he pulled his car out of the parking spot and drove up the ramp.

Women! There weren't many who were worth much. Come to think of it, there weren't that many nice guys, either. He was one of the few.

Whistling in tune with the music on the radio, he drove home, proud that he had been able to quell the woman next to him with such a mild word like *persimmon*. He'd even been chivalrous, whether she'd admit it or not, having walked her to her car.

Now he hoped he never ran into her again. Women like that were too much trouble.

By the time he was in his town house and stretched out on his oversize couch, a Scotch in his hand and his eyes drifting shut as he listened to the late-night news, his mind was occupied with other things besides the events at the Music Hall.

The woman in the black skirt with the persimmon mind was just an incident to be forgotten.

When the phone rang and he listened to his answering machine pick it up, she came back—vividly.

"Leo? Are you home yet, buddy? This is Sam, and I'm hoping you enjoyed the little surprise I had sitting next to you at the musical tonight. Let me know how it went, okay?" There was a click as Sam hung up.

Leo took another drink of his Scotch. It was a setup, after all. It wasn't an old friend of Sam's, or even a friend of a friend. It was a setup. One that failed badly.

Finally he couldn't stand it anymore and dialed Sam's number, only to get his answering machine.

Damn these contraptions! They were wonderful if you didn't feel like talking or weren't home, but Leo hated his calls being recorded on one. Still, there wasn't much he could do about it.

"Sam. Call me right back. I have a bone to pick with you, my friend." He punctuated his order with a slam of the phone. Sam had been a friend since law school. And since those days they had remained good buddies, until now. This might be the splitting of the ways, if Sam had really tried to pull a fast one.

Sam dialed back almost immediately. "What's up?" he said in a voice that could be described as innocent.

"Who was that woman you gave Catherine's ticket to?" Leo asked without preamble.

"Oh, she got to you, did she?" Sam sounded highly pleased. "She's my secretary, Brenda, and she's a treasure. I've always thought the two of you should meet, but she was always chasing down paperwork or on an errand when you visited my office. Not that you drop by that often."

Leo took a deep breath. "And she knew who I was?"

"No, I didn't tell either one of you. Why?" Sam sounded puzzled now.

"Because she did know who I was and took an almost instant dislike to me. I couldn't figure out what I had done wrong, but if she's your secretary, she probably knows more about me than I do myself."

"Are you saying I gossiped about you, Leo?" Sam's voice became tight.

Leo sighed, running a large hand through his sandy blond hair. "No, I'm saying that she'd probably overheard you and April talking about me and put two and two together to make zero." Sam and his law partner, April, were as close as two friends could be. They usually talked everything over together.

Sam whistled through his teeth. "You might have a point, Leo. Brenda's in on half our conversations," he said thoughtfully. "Anyway, she's had a hard time lately, and I just thought that you two would hit it off. Sorry if you had a bad time of it. I forget that Brenda doesn't like too many men."

"What happened?" Leo told himself that he asked for politeness's sake, but his interest was piqued. It would be easier to understand her actions tonight if he could place her in a neat little box with a label.

"Her husband walked out on her over three years ago. Left her for another woman—younger, richer and no children. Brenda's got three. Since then she's had to work and be a single parent to those little hellions. I don't think it's been easy."

"And that's the reason she took it out on me?" Leo's voice was mocking.

"No. She probably knows your reputation and the fact that you enjoy the, uh, female sex without commitment."

"She's a bitter woman."

"Perhaps," Sam conceded. "But she's a delight to talk to, with a wonderful wit and a warm heart."

"Sounds like a blind date I once had in high school," Leo said dryly. "And I didn't care for her, either."

"Backfired on me, huh?"

"You bet."

"Damn," Sam muttered. "I can hear her now. She's gonna chew me out good."

"Your tough luck, Sam. You never could control the women in your life. Just look at the mess you've made of it," Leo said, chuckling, knowing well Sam's love for women, especially one in particular—his wife of just a few months.

And for some reason that Leo didn't try very hard to pin down, he felt that he owed Brenda an apology. "Give me her address, will you, Sam? I'll send her some flowers and pretend that the rudeness was my fault. Maybe that will get you off the hook."

"Great," Sam said heartily, and by the tone of his voice, Leo knew that Sam saw right through him and had decided to let him play this silly game.

By the time Leo hung up the phone he was exhausted. He *knew* that he should never get involved with women who had problems. And this proved it. It was so much easier for him to get together with a woman he had nothing in common with. Someone who only wanted fun and sex with no loving little sounds of commitment getting in the way.

The perennial bachelor.

That thought wasn't as reassuring as it used to be.

2

BRENDA WAS BACK IN CONTROL of her emotions by the time she drove out of the underground parking garage. There was a definite chill in the air, she thought as she drove the downtown streets to reach the freeway. Shivering, she knew she should have thought to bring a coat or at least a sweater. When she had left home earlier, the weather had been nice. But she should have known better, especially with her itchy throat. Thanksgiving was just over a month away and this was the season for quick changes in the weather.

The Volvo wheezed along the freeway, practically driving itself as Brenda became lost in thought. So that was Leo Coulter. She remembered something, that April had once whimsically described him as being a giant, cuddly teddy bear with the most honest, sweetest disposition this side of the Mississippi.

Huh! April had forgot to mention that he was as deadly as an invisible virus floating in the air. He had too much of everything! Too much virility, too much sex appeal, too much good looks.

In one way she was embarrassed because of how rude she had acted toward him, but she justified it by remembering his history of tall, long-legged redheads with bigger eyes than brains. He deserved what he got.

She pulled up the driveway of her home, not stopping until she reached the closed garage door. It was a beautiful old neighborhood and hers was a beautiful old house. One-story stucco, it was done in tans and stark white. She and David had bought the place with the idea of fixing it up and selling it again. They had almost finished the project when he had walked out the door and into another woman's arms.

By the time she parked the car in the garage, she was sneezing. By the time she hit the door, she was blowing her nose. By the time Mrs. Endicott, the baby-sitter, left, she was feverish.

Good grief! Maybe that hulk of a man really was a virus!

She tiptoed into Kingsley's room and stared down at the young boy. Young. He was eleven now and firmly believed that he should be the man in the family, but was frightened by what that might mean. He was so young to try to be so strong. And that was her blessing. He looked exactly like his father, only his father was all smiles and sweetness outside with no depth where it counted. Kingsley had depth. He worried about his sisters, his mother, the house. He was a born worrier.

She brushed the dark brown hair from his forehead and gave him a whisper-light kiss. He mumbled something, then turned over and curled into a fetal position.

The next room held her two daughters. All pink confection and white lace, it was an adorable little girl's room. That was the problem. Maggie, ten, and Janie, seven, had almost outgrown the little-girl decor but there was nothing she could do about it. There was hardly enough money to keep the family going. She leaned over the first twin canopied bed and gave Maggie a kiss. Her dark brown hair was in tangles from tossing her head back and forth on the pillow in sleepy agitation. Like Kingsley, she believed that she was supposed to be a substitute mother when Brenda was at work.

She bumped her shin as she rounded one bed to reach the other. Janie was sprawled on her back, her arms flung out to the sides, a small, sweet smile on her face. Of the three of them, Janie was the most uninhibited one in the group. Her sister and brother catered to her whims, attempting in some way to give her the childhood they didn't consciously know was taken from them. Consequently she was slightly on the spoiled side and thoroughly charming.

Closing the door behind her, Brenda walked to the bathroom. She took two aspirin, then went to bed, thankful that it was Friday and she didn't have to work tomorrow.

Tomorrow would be a better day.

BRENDA HAD BEEN WRONG. Tomorrow was lousy. Her head felt like an overstuffed pillow, her throat was burning as if someone had stuck a hot poker down it, her eyes were swollen and her nose wouldn't stop running. Definitely a touch of flu, she decided. She looked in the mirror and made a sound of disgust. She not only felt awful, but she looked worse.

She could hear the children arguing about which box of cereal they would use. Janie's voice rose another octave in a whine that had been practiced to perfection. Brenda held her ears as she weaved her way into the kitchen.

"Oh, Momma!" Maggie wailed. "You were supposed to be asleep. I'm making a surprise for you!"

"In that case, I think I'll go back to bed," Brenda said, seeing that although there was a mess to clean later, no one was bloody or in need of first aid. Anything less could wait to be handled until she felt better. She gave a wan smile and left, hoping against hope that the yellow goop in the pan wasn't meant to be pancakes for her.

They were, and she ate two before her stomach revolted. Downing more aspirin and closing her eyes, she gave last-minute instructions, then blessed the sleep that pulled her away from everything, including the pain.

She didn't awaken again until three, when she heard Janie's wail fill the house like a banshee's keen would fill the countryside. Running and stumbling into the living room, Brenda found Janie trying to punch Kingsley's midsection; only his hand on her forehead kept her at a distance.

"What's going on here?" Brenda croaked, hoping she was putting enough sternness in her voice. No one glanced her way. Maggie, trying to be the diplomat, was pulling on Janie's shoulders, and Brenda could see coming the blow that Maggie would receive in her ribs as Janie once more reared back to land a punch to Kingsley's stomach.

Brenda took a deep breath, quickly pushed Maggie aside so the blow would only graze her ribs and stood

with hands on hips as three pairs of big brown eyes
turned toward her. Silence hung in the air. Even Janie
had instantly stopped the wailing.

But before Brenda could speak, a chorus of young
voices filled the air, all explaining at the same time.

"Mom, Janie wouldn't..."

"Momma, they won't let me..."

"Mother, Janie's being a little..."

"Hush!" Brenda cried, holding her ears and closing
her eyes, praying the thudding in her head wasn't the
sign of an aneurysm that would stop her dead in her
tracks.

Then feeling guilty because she had almost lost her
temper with the children, who were out of sorts because she was ill, she smiled, hoping they couldn't see
the strain she was under. "Now, one at a time, please
tell me what's going on."

They did. Janie had wanted to wake her mother to
show her the flowers that had just been delivered.
Maggie and Kingsley had tried to stop her. Result: the
argument. Using all her concentration and filling in
between the lines, it only took Brenda five minutes to
half understand what was going on.

"What flowers?" she asked, confused.

All three stepped away from the coffee table. There
in the center was the most enormous, beautiful spring
bouquet of cut flowers she had ever seen. A tall brass
vase was filled with yellow rosebuds, surrounded by
pink and white tulips. Around them were pale laven-
der daisies and then large, deep purple irises and sun-
golden daffodils. It was gorgeous. "But..." she began,
only to be interrupted by Janie.

"Read the card, Mommy. Read it out loud!"

She opened the envelope and glanced at the card, skipping to the signature. Leo Coulter. Her lips thinned. So he thought she was owed an apology. Like hell. He did it knowing that she was probably at fault and this was his way of making her feel even more embarrassed over her thoughtless behavior. That damn man!

When questions assailed her, she answered through gritted teeth. "It was a gentleman who sat next to me at the musical last night. He took both armrests and because it was rude to do so, he apologized," she said, hoping that there was a moral or lesson in manners in her explanation that would detract them enough for her to go back to bed.

There was, and she did.

She closed her eyes, snuggled down in the covers and drifted off to sleep. The last thing she remembered was the sharp color of hazel-green eyes as they narrowed their gaze on her.

LEO DRESSED in a dark brown three-piece suit and royal-blue-and-brown striped tie. He checked himself over in the bedroom's full-length mirror and nodded his head, then went into the living room to pour himself a drink before picking up his date. Her name was Rhoda and she was a cello player with the Los Angeles Symphony. That's why he had accepted Sam's ticket last night. She was one of the best musicians in her field and absolutely brilliant when it came to music. But after the subject of music was exhausted, there wasn't much to discuss that they might have in common, which left a very satisfactory physical relationship to explore. No emotional commitment or entwined lives and careers.

Just what he wanted.

She agreed that his idea of a wonderful evening was dining in a good restaurant, then being seen in one of the better nightclubs in the city. She didn't seem to care if Leo talked his head off or remained silent the entire evening. Her answer to his words or silence was the same; she just looked at him with limpid blue eyes, shook her long red hair and smiled a lot. She was no more interested in law than he was in the politics of being a member of a symphony orchestra. Undemanding, that was Rhoda. Besides, there was something very sexy about a woman in a dress sitting on a stage with a cello between her legs. Something Freudian called to him.

Sam used to like undemanding women, too, but then for deeper conversation he had his partner April Flynn-Sullivan to spar with. Then he met country singer Catherine Sinclair and fell head over heels for the petite blonde with the sharp tongue. They fell in love instantly, it seemed to Leo, and finally married a few months ago. They had the best of both worlds, good looks, sharp minds and diverse careers. They made a perfect match....

He drank down his Scotch and practically slammed the heavy glass tumbler on the bar.

His heart wasn't in going out. He didn't want to stay home, either, otherwise he would have canceled the date with no regrets. He didn't know what the hell he wanted, so he might as well go along with the original plan to take Rhoda out on the town.

Grabbing his coat, he walked out.

It was only after Leo had warmed up the car and left the driveway that he remembered Brenda. Early this morning he had ordered flowers sent to her, the largest bouquet they could make that wouldn't look like a funeral arrangement. She should have received them and his note of apology this afternoon.

He wondered what she thought of his gesture. Did she like the flowers? Or did she hate them because they came from him? It took mental effort he hadn't wanted to expend for him to predict how women might react; that's why he always chose the undemanding ones. It was easier. He saved his second guessing for his law practice.

He headed toward Rhoda's house, taking the freeway. As he glanced up he saw the exit that, if memory served him correctly, would take him to Brenda's address.

Without thinking twice, he pulled over two lanes and headed for the exit. Questions shouted in his mind but he ignored them as he headed toward Brenda's.

He cruised the street, finally finding the number. He never asked himself why he had memorized the address. He didn't want to know the answer.

Parking the car by the curb, he glanced at his watch. He had another half hour before he was due at Rhoda's. That would give him time to make his unnecessary apology in person to Brenda and see what her reaction was.

But the doorbell brought three pairs of brown eyes peering up at him as the door was fully opened. The two oldest had red lipstick zigzagged on their fore-

heads and cheeks. The littlest one had her hair in what
was supposed to be braids. Perched on her head was a
sunbonnet that had seen better days . . . years ago.

"Is your mom here?" he asked, a smile tugging at his
mouth as he saw the oldest, a boy, step forward as if to
guard his sisters.

"Yes, sir, but she can't come to the door right now,"
he said solemnly. "Can I help?"

"I'm Leo Coulter, and I just stopped by to see if your
mother received my flowers and card this afternoon,"
Leo explained equally solemnly. What in the hell was
Brenda so busy doing that she would allow three children to open wide a door to a stranger? This was Los
Angeles, not *Little House on the Prairie*, for goodness'
sake!

The littlest girl grinned, showing two front teeth
missing and an absolutely charming gleam in her eye.
"Are you the one who said he was sorry?" she asked,
lisping slightly.

The middle child's elbow came out just far enough
to touch the little one, silencing her, even though she
obviously had other questions to ask.

Leo couldn't help it; he had to smile. So Brenda had
told them what his card said. "Yes, I am. I'm afraid I was
a little rude last night and thought your mother deserved an apology."

Despite the elbow digging Maggie had given her,
Janie decided he needed an answer. "Yes," she lisped.
"And you also tried to take the armrests away from
Momma. That wasn't nice."

My God, did she tell the kids everything? He took a deep breath. "That's why I sent the flowers. Now, may I come in so I can speak to your momma?"

With obvious reluctance the three children moved aside from the doorway and allowed him entrance. The boy was the leader. He held out his small hand. "My name is Kingsley and I'm the oldest." Leo shook hands, trying desperately to keep his expression as grave as the situation seemed to call for. Kingsley continued, "This is my sister Maggie and my sister Janie. Won't you have a seat in the living room and I'll see if Mom's awake."

Until that moment, Leo had not looked around, but as he stepped into the living room, his eyes widened. The kids had obviously been making a tent with newspapers. The same zigzag patterns that were on their faces were also on the newspapers, which had been taped together. To the side was a stack of telephone books with a statue of a Tang horse in front of it. The room was the worst disaster Leo had ever seen. In the corner was his flower arrangement, half picked over, standing on the floor.

"I see she received the flowers," he said dryly.

"Oh, yeth," Janie crooned. "And we're pretenen' that they're a whole field of flowers and I'm a girl on a wagon train west and Kingsley is the Indian chief." Her eyes were wide with excitement.

Leo couldn't help the deep dark chuckle that began to rumble in his throat. So that explained it. Cowboys and Indians. "And what part does Maggie play?"

"She's the wagon master," Janie explained earnestly, disregarding her sibling's acute embarrassment.

Kingsley, still standing in the doorway, stood tall. "Mother said that it was up to me to keep the girls happy, so I'm playing a silly game with them. Girls only know silly games." His disdain was apparent, as well as the fact that he had truly been enjoying the game. Leo didn't know much about kids, but something told him that the girls wouldn't paint the tepee with lipstick on their own.

"I see," Leo said. "And where is your mother while you're keeping the girls happy?"

Maggie leaned down and picked up the horse, which Leo now understood to be the team that kept the wagon train going. She cradled it in her arms as if it were a doll.

"She's indisposable right now."

"Indisposable?"

"Yes. She can't get out of bed unless it's an emergency. She's sick. She has the flu."

"Isn't there someone who can watch out for you, help clean and cook?"

Kingsley looked insulted. "We can take care of ourselves. We're not babies, you know," he said haughtily.

"No, but wouldn't it be better if you didn't have someone to take care of and could play games just because you wanted to?" Leo asked quietly, his mind turning over the facts he now knew. "I'll tell you what," he went on, not waiting for an answer. "I'll be the adult that helps. If you guys promise to clean this up later, I'll take care of the dinner and your mother. Okay?"

Three heads nodded at once, smiles breaking out as they watched him stride from the living room and down the hall toward the kitchen.

Disaster met him there, too. Spilled cereal was crusted to the table, some kind of butter was stuck to and dribbled down the stove, the cabinets were opened and half their contents spilled on the floor.

First things first. He'd check on Brenda. Somehow the impression he had received of her last night, coupled with what Sam had told him didn't jibe with this scene. Unless she was really ill.

He found her in the first bedroom down the hall. She was sprawled on her stomach wearing an old T-shirt and a brief pair of ivory panties. Apparently she had gotten hot, for the sheets and blankets were pushed to the foot of the bed. Her nose was red and her cheeks wore flags of color from her fever, making her freckles stand out in relief. He had been right about her legs. They were neither as long nor as thin as he usually went for, but they were soft and . . . pliable. A very nice set. Her bottom was gently rounded and sort of perky looking. He already knew how it bounced just slightly when she walked on those high-heeled spikes she had worn last night.

He almost wished she'd turn over so he could see if his eyes had deceived him about the fullness of her breasts. Dropping that thought because of where it would lead, he laid a hand on her forehead and then went directly to the bathroom to find aspirin. It was on the counter, the cap off. Alongside it was a half-filled glass of water.

Without hesitating he refilled the glass and grabbed two of the white pills. Now to get them down her without having her go into a fit at the sight of him.

It turned out to be no trouble at all.

"Brenda," he whispered softly in her ear. "Turn over and take some more aspirin, honey. You have a fever."

As if she did it all the time, she immediately obeyed him. Keeping her eyes closed, she took the aspirin, popped them in her mouth and sipped the water he held to her lips. Then, giving a soft moan, she curled up, breathing deeply once before settling back into a heavy sleep.

Leo watched her for a few moments. Despite her sharp tongue, there was something about her that made him feel protective. Perhaps it was the vulnerability of her position. Or the vulnerability of her private life. He pulled the covers up around her, tucking the sheet under her chin.

Suddenly he felt like an intruder.

Carefully getting up from the edge of the bed, he tried to tiptoe from the room. A grin split his face. Who was he kidding? He was too big a hulk to tiptoe, and she was too far gone in sleep to care how much noise anyone made! Still, he closed the door very gently.

Now what? He couldn't very well leave her and the children here to their own devices. His thoughts of checking on Brenda and then ordering hamburgers for the kids before leaving flew out of his mind. The children looked as if they were enough to handle when she was well, let alone now. And she couldn't even cope with taking aspirin on time, never mind keeping an eye on the Indians in the other room. Whether he liked it or not, he felt obligated to stay. It was the punishment he gave himself for coming over here uninvited in the first place.

At least finding the telephone wasn't a problem; it hung on the kitchen wall where nothing short of a coat could cover it up.

He kept telling himself over and over that there was only one thing he could do, caught in the position he was; and that was to call off his date and stay with the kids. After all, it wasn't the kids' fault their mother was ill, and it wasn't Leo's fault that such nice kids had such a waspy mother. He'd chalk this up to his good deed for the week.

He was able to explain just enough to Rhoda to let him off the hook gracefully. It sounded a lot like that old story, nursing a sick friend, but it couldn't be helped. No matter how light the relationship, canceling a date this late was rude, and he was grateful that she didn't seem to mind too much.

It took a good hour for him to clean the kitchen enough so that he could plan and cook a meal. The kitchen was large, but the oval table in the center took away a lot of the walk space, so that he felt cramped moving his bulk around in the same area that Brenda usually moved in.

Taking an inventory of the food wasn't easy. First he had to figure out where she kept everything. He found package after package of ground beef, all with sale stickers on them. There were loads of noodles and two or three cans of each vegetable, apparently bought in groups, and even a few prepackaged items. And fresh fruit.

"Damn," he muttered under his breath. He thought he had forever given up meals like this when he finally passed his bar exam. Instead, Brenda bought groceries like the ones he used to buy: the best you could get for the least amount of money and still have a balanced meal. And he was stuck with it. It just wasn't feasible to go to the grocery store and leave the Indians here, and he'd be damned if he'd take them along. His experience didn't run that far, but his fear did. He'd seen harried mothers in the stores trying to control their own kids, so how could he expect to control someone else's?

And he had promised himself that once he was in his own practice, he'd never eat anything that wasn't steak, fish or written on highly priced menus. He gave a heavy sigh. "Macaroni and beef, it is," he said under his breath, hoping that the salad he could make would take away the imaginary taste of poverty he knew so well.

By the time dinner was cooked, he had the Indians turning back into kids. It took a lot of effort, but with the help of Brenda's cold cream the lipstick finally washed off their faces. The newspapers were picked up, the telephone books put away for another day and everything was straightened back to what Leo hoped was normal.

By the time the kitchen was cleaned, the kids were in bed and Leo had been coerced into reading four stories, it was well past eleven.

For an evening like this he had given up dining and dancing with the beautiful Rhoda. He had given up his water bed filled with a redhead he could murmur directions to and know they'd be obeyed. He had given up relaxing with good brandy and slim legs. Sometimes his actions didn't make much sense. Neither did his choices for a fun Saturday night.

Thank God Sam couldn't see him now or he'd laugh his head off!

One more time Leo tiptoed in, gave a still-groggy Brenda her aspirin and then, with a bone-weary exhaustion he hadn't felt in a long time, he lay back on the couch to watch the news. After that he would leave. After that . . . The last completed thought in his head brought the first deep snore from the confines of his throat.

BRENDA AWOKE and rolled over. The digital clock at her bedside said 6:29. Was that A.M. or P.M.? She squinted at the window and decided that it could be either.

And she was starved.

The kids! What had happened to the children? As quickly as she could, she got out of bed and practically flew down the hall, checking in each room. All three children were in bed, their pajamas on, their rooms picked up. She leaned against the doorjamb of Kingsley's room and glanced from him to the girls' room across the hall. Would wonders never cease? Kingsley and Maggie had taken care of everything, including the cleaning, if their rooms were anything to go by.

She felt her forehead. She still had a low-grade fever, but she felt tons better than she had yesterday. It was just the twenty-four-hour flu, thank goodness. With luck she'd be well enough to go to work Monday. She couldn't afford to miss one dollar of her paycheck, not that Sam wasn't generous. It just cost so much to live.

She walked into the kitchen, vague memories of coming in here yesterday still playing in her mind. Yesterday it had been a disaster, but this morning it was clean as a whistle with the exception of a lone glass in the sink. She leaned down to stare at the table. Nope, nothing there. They must have had to scrub hard to get rid of the dried cereal they had spilled.

Tears stung her eyes. Bless their little hearts. Ever since David had left them and she had gone back to work, they had tried so hard to help. Last night only proved how much they had been forced to grow up and she hated that thought. She hated David for making them do it.

She made coffee, staring out the kitchen window while it perked. The large oaks were barren of their leaves, the ground covered with them. The sky was gradually lightening up enough to indicate that it would be an overcast day.

When the coffee was ready, she poured a mugful and sipped on it as she slowly walked down the hall toward the living room. That would probably be a disaster area after the kids playing in it yesterday. She smiled. But they had done so well everywhere else that it didn't matter. They had too little time to be kids that she could afford to let them loose once in a while.

She stopped at the entrance to the living room, as if there were an invisible wall.

The room was perfectly clean. And there was a man, a very big man in a white shirt and dark brown pants snoring his way to Shangri-la on her couch.

She had been right. This was the room with the disaster.

3

SO MANY THOUGHTS flew through Brenda's mind at once. What was *he* doing here? Why was he here? She had to get him out before her children saw him! Never had she allowed a man to spend the night in her home! Never! Good grief. She didn't even know a man she could have invited to stay here! And the last thought— how did she get him *out* of here without anyone knowing, so she wouldn't be the scandal of the neighborhood?

He stirred, turned, then fell into a deep sleep again, a frown marring his forehead. Brenda couldn't help the smile that forced its way into her eyes. That big hulk must have been as uncomfortable as could be on that particular couch. It looked all right, but it was so unpleasant to sleep on that even she wouldn't do it. Soft cushions, hard seams with ironlike binding, a sag on two sides instead of the middle where any decent couch would give; these all played a monsterlike part in making those who chose it for sleep, miserable.

Well, the only way for her to find out what to do next was to wake the sleeping dragon.

She bent down to within inches of his ear. "Mr. Coulter, wake up, please," she said in a very soft but firm voice.

He stirred, the frown disappearing as another definitely more pleasant thought played through his dreams.

"Mr. Coulter," she said more loudly.

He smiled, his lips turning up delightfully in the corners. He had such a wonderfully tender smile for such a big bear of a man. She dropped that thought.

"Mr. Coulter!"

Eyes flickered on that one. Golden brows moved up and down once. Then heavy lids lifted to show their treasure of hazel green. He stared directly at her, but she knew he didn't really see her. He saw something else, something that he was dreaming, perhaps. Once more he smiled, demonstrating just how easily his smile could charm, even in sleep. Damn him!

"What are you doing here?" she asked slowly, as if speaking to a child. "You're not supposed to be here."

"Mmm, was I sleeping?" he asked groggily, not moving. He just continued to look up at her, a small smile still etched in the corners of his mouth. His eyes leisurely traveled her face, glancing at her red nose, then her slim throat and moving down to the vee of her old yellow T-shirt. His gaze skipped the decal that hid her unbound breasts and latched on to her legs. Lovely legs. Even if they weren't as long as he was accustomed to.

Brenda sighed with impatience, finally straightening. It was a mistake, for his eyes immediately moved back to the logo of her T-shirt, where the thin material defined the thrust of her pert breasts. "Yes, I think you were sleeping. But only you can answer that, along with a few other questions I'd like to ask."

With a moan, then a small grunt, he pulled himself to an upright position. "You do know, don't you, that this couch could have been used in Salem for testing witches? It's the perfect punishment." His deep voice, though not loud, echoed through her nervous system and ran all the way down to her toes. "I've never slept on anything more uncomfortable in my life, including the rocky ground."

"How interesting that you've made a study of sleeping places," she echoed, but decided not to push her luck when she saw the narrow-eyed look he gave her. "It isn't meant for sleeping," she said just as sweetly so he wouldn't realize that she was retreating. "It's meant to look nice. If I had wanted a bed in here, I would have bought one." She left out the fact that she had bought it for a low price, hoping one day to replace it.

"Congratulations. You've answered one of my questions. You don't normally have friends stay over, at least not the sort who sleep on couches." His voice was dry, his hazel eyes beginning to twinkle with merriment.

She stiffened at his barb. "No one stays over, Mr. Coulter. If I had wanted you to stay over, I would have asked. I don't believe I did."

"No," he admitted slowly, "your children did. Janie even offered me her bed, but I graciously turned it down. I didn't think you'd approve, to say nothing of a man my size and age sleeping up to his eyeballs in pink and white ruffles. It would destroy my image."

"I'd like to destroy a few things myself. Could you possibly explain to an innocent bystander what you're doing here?" she asked patiently, trying desperately to curb her tongue. It wasn't working well, but he'd never guess just how caustic she could get. "I don't remember inviting you here, nor do I remember admitting you to my home." It was as plain as could be that if he had come to the door she probably would've slammed it in his face!

"Your children let me in. They asked if I was the man who sent the flowers and I told them I was," he said into his lap as he ran his hands through his tousled hair, then rubbed the thick cords of his neck and tried to wake up. She watched his every movement. "Do you have more of that coffee you're holding, or is that the only cup in the house?"

"There's more in the kitchen." Brenda turned and marched from the room, hoping he would think she was going to the kitchen and follow her. What she really needed was a robe and headed for her room to get one. It didn't matter that the only robe she now had was a terrible, chenille, green thing, which made her look like a faded spring flower that had lost all its petals. That's the way she usually felt, anyway.

She grabbed her robe from the closet and practically threw it on, tying the sash as quickly as possible. She only gave a glance in the mirror, knowing beforehand that her nose would be red, her eyes splotchy, her hair mussed. But she would be damned if she would straighten herself up for him.

One more quick check on the children, who were still sleeping soundly, and she was on her way to the kitchen.

Leo stood sipping on a large mug of coffee, his hips resting against the counter. She tried to hide her grin.

It was the mug that said "World's Greatest Mom." He certainly didn't fit the image! She wouldn't allow herself to dwell on the image he did fit.

"Find it?" she asked as if she hadn't seen his evidence.

"Yes, even if it is weak and you're out of milk," he muttered, gulping down more.

"I have milk," she stated.

"No, you don't. I used it up last night when I made dinner."

She ignored that. "Now would you please explain to me what you're doing here and how you got in?" She thought her voice held a great deal of patience.

He thought she was losing patience rapidly. Well, so was he. Some good Boy Scout deed! "I came by to see if you received my flowers," he said archly. "The house was in an uproar. The kids had lipstick from one ear to the other. They had painted their faces like Indians, and there were newspapers strewen from the hall to the living room, to say nothing of the mess in the kitchen. I saw that you were sick, canceled my date and took care of you and your children."

Leo held up his hand as if she was about to interrupt. "No, don't thank me. Your kind concern about my sleeping arrangements was enough to warm the cockles of my heart." Her dirty look made him give a heavy sigh before continuing the explanation. "Sometime late last night, after making sure that the kids were asleep, I sat on the couch to get my bearings before I left. I fell asleep. End of story." His tone was short and clipped, telling Brenda just how irritated he was with the entire situation.

Ignoring the fact that he had gone out of his way to help her, she allowed her anger to flare. *She* hadn't asked him to cancel his date. *She* hadn't even asked him to drop by. The nerve of him blaming her for his miserable night! Vaguely, in the back of her mind, she now recalled someone giving her aspirin and a cool cloth for her head, but she hadn't been awake enough to bother worrying about it. Now her ire was up.

She stood as straight as she could, her eyes flashing dangerously. "No one in this family asked for your help, Mr. Coulter. I don't even remember being nice enough to you for you to expect a welcome here," she gritted through her teeth. "My family and I have been able to weather other crises, and I'm sure we could have weathered this one without your help," she lied, although she knew why the house was so clean and the children in bed...in pajamas. But that wasn't the point, she kept telling herself. "Now, if you don't mind, I'd like you to leave. There is nothing for you here. No long-legged redhead, no simpletons, no women who can't do without a man to lean on."

His dark brows rose skeptically. "Are you sure? From what I saw yesterday, your Indians were ready to burn the wagons before retreating."

He was calling her a simpleton. A woman who needed a man. The nerve of him! Since when did he have a Ph.D. in child rearing and family life? "If I needed anyone, it certainly wouldn't be you. You're on the other side of the rock from where I live, and I'm not sure I'd like my children contaminated by your values and ideas." Her voice was low and icy cold, a blast of wind almost freezing the very air.

Leo's hazel-green eyes widened. He drank down the rest of the coffee in one gulp, slammed his mug on the counter and walked to the living room. Grabbing his coat and tie, he headed toward the front door. It almost opened in Brenda's face as she followed close behind.

Her reflexes weren't as sharp as they used to be, for when he wheeled around and grabbed her by her small shoulders, then kissed the hell out of her, she didn't move. His mouth moved over hers as if he were the conqueror and she the helpless maiden. And she was. Fire shot down to curl her bare toes, but her hands dangled helplessly by her sides.

"You're right," he muttered, taking a deep breath when his lips left hers. "You don't need a man, you need a large bonfire to melt the wall of ice you've built around yourself. No man could compete with that." And he left, slamming the door in her face.

Suddenly propelled into action, Brenda put her fingers to her now-swollen lips. Breathlessly she ran to the front window, watching his progress through the sheer curtains.

His steps down the front walk were deliberate yet graceful. His eyes, when he scanned the front window of her living room, were narrowed. His smile, when he turned and waved at her most gossipy neighbor, was wide.

Brenda placed her shaking hands over her face. The neighbors had seen him leaving at—she checked her watch with a feeling of fatality that was all-consuming—seven-thirty. Los Angeles might be the most swinging city of the ages, but her neighborhood was as stodgy as they came. They had talked about her divorce for a year. Now she had even given them something else to talk about...her love life, which had been nonexistent until today. Technically it still was, but who would believe her? After that front-door kiss and his leaving with coat and tie in hand this early in the morning? No one!

She wanted to cry, but as usual the tears wouldn't come, only the ache in her throat and the burning sensation in her eyes testified to her state of despair.

There was no doubt about it, Leo Coulter had turned her life upside down by coming here. She hoped she never, ever, saw him again! Damn him! Damn all men!

Still, her fingers clung to her lips, the lips he had touched with his own.

LEO DROVE OFF with his hands clenching the steering wheel as if it were Brenda's shoulders. If he could, he would have shaken her to kingdom come, then tossed her aside and forgotten her.

But he couldn't

If he had been smart, he never would have kissed her, stirring up feelings in them both.

But he had.

He remembered his thoughts about Brenda when he had been talking to Sam on the phone. He had figured she needed help, some kind of counseling. But he had been wrong.

They both did.

With a heavy sigh, Leo dragged himself out of the car and up the walk to his house. He opened the door and, for just a moment, stood in the front entrance looking around. It was a good house: spacious, great for entertaining, light and airy. No paper tents, no uncomfortable couches, no mess. Not even cereal littered the kitchen counter. It was also very empty.

He shrugged his shoulders and, despite the early hour, reached in the refrigerator and grabbed a beer.

Boy! Was he lucky! He had women, wine and song whenever he wanted it. He didn't have to put up with whining, sick women and children who thought the West was yet to be won. Yup, real lucky.

And he was going to stay that way.

By midafternoon Leo had showered, shaved, drunk two more beers and still had plenty of time to pace the length of his living room. There were so many things he could do the rest of his day, that he didn't know which to choose.

He could call Rhoda and see her this afternoon, perhaps hop into bed and get rid of this pent-up energy he seemed to be brimful of.

He could visit Sam and Catherine and listen to them discuss the newest methods of delivery.

He could go to Jace and April's and listen to the cacophony the triplets made.

He could go to his favorite bar and watch the afternoon football game with the guys.

He could go to Brenda's, maybe with pizzas in hand, and apologize for his bad behavior this morning. He could also check on the kids and make sure they were okay.

Leo stopped his pacing. There was no doubt about it; he was certifiably crazy. The woman all but threw him out of her house and life. In fact she'd done everything but write on a blackboard a hundred times that she hated him. Yet he still wanted to get into the fray with her, which would probably rival World War III predictions.

But he had no choice. Not really. For Sam's sake he had to help smooth over the boner he had pulled. He wasn't sure what it was, but at this point if Brenda was willing to make him feel guilty, he'd feel it. Anything for Sam, old buddy, who had to work with that she-wolf day in and day out.

This would be his last act of appeasement since the flowers didn't work.

Leo reached for the phone book. The list of pizza parlors near her neighborhood were few, which made it easy to pick up the phone and dial one. How many pizzas for a family of five—well, four and himself— would he need? "I'd like four pizzas, all different, please," he found himself ordering, telling them that he'd be there in half an hour. That was without observing speed limits.

He was out the door in thirty seconds.

He chuckled to himself. And they said large men couldn't move fast!

BRENDA WIPED THE COUNTER one more time, then laid the dishcloth over the edge of the sink. They had had hamburgers, again, for lunch and she had bribed the children to play outside for a while with the promise of cookie making this afternoon if they would give her time to clean up the kitchen in peace. They had agreed and were now playing outside, their jackets open and their whoops of fun echoing between the houses as they participated in a game of tag with the neighbor's children.

She sniffled. Her bout of flu was going almost as quickly as it had come, thank goodness. She said a quick prayer that the children wouldn't catch it, for it would mean at least one or two days out of school for each child and she would have to take time off work to be with them. That meant she could be out as much as six days. With Christmas just a couple of months away, she really couldn't afford that.

She glanced out the window again. The children were too busy having fun to want to come in right now. Good. She could work on her coupon redemption and contest system for a while. Who knows? Someday she might even win one of the contests she entered all the time. Anything could happen, but the little voice in her head said, it usually didn't . . . to her.

Taking the shoe box of coupons from the shelf in her closet, she began making her shopping list for next week. If she was careful, taking double coupons and sales into consideration, she could get by with less than half the grocery bills that others had for a family this large. It just took so much planning that she had to reserve a half day for the list alone.

Halfway through her chore, a frown etched on her brow, she heard the doorbell ring. At the same time she could hear the children whooping in eagerness and delight. What for?

But when she opened the front door, she knew why.

The blond giant stood in the midst of six or seven children holding four extra-large pizza boxes over his head, a warm, heart-tugging grin on his mouth and a definite twinkling lighting his eyes.

"Hi," he said softly, and she heard his voice above the yells as if it was whispered directly in her ear. But her mind wouldn't work beyond that word and she couldn't seem to move again. "Can I come in before they gang up on me?"

Her nod was abrupt, but her eyes glinted with mischief as she realized that he looked like Gulliver with all the little people trying to tie him down. He must have been reading her mind because he grinned, too, as he made his way through the doorway and toward the kitchen.

She followed behind with the kids, watching his lithe movements as he took the pizzas from above his head and set them on the counter. When he turned, his hazel gaze pinned her to the floor. "I was watching TV when I had this craving for pizza. Then I remembered a certain young man who said it was his second favorite meal," he teased, glancing at Kingsley.

"I did not, Leo! I said I loved it first! Mom's hamburgers were second! I remember!" Kingsley exclaimed before he began blushing, suddenly understanding why Leo had said what he did. "But they're pretty close, Leo." Now the boy's round eyes twinkled as he hugged Brenda around the waist. "Pretty close!"

"It's Mr. Coulter to you, my man," she said sternly. Brenda ruffled his hair, a softened look coming over her face that warmed Leo's heart. Why couldn't she look at him that way? "You, my friend, are turning into a real con artist," she said, chuckling, and Kingsley grinned back, looking more boyish than Leo had seen him before. Something flashed between the two of them, and Leo was once more a spectator, feeling left outside some window to stare in at a moment of happiness.

He cleared his throat. "What kind do you like, King?" he asked, praying the restaurant had given him whatever it was.

"The big special with *everything!*"

Leo smiled. "Then you're in luck. I've got one." He turned to the two girls. "And what kind do the wagon master and the flower girl like?" he teased.

"Pepperoni! Pepperoni!" Janie said as she jumped up and down in time to her own words.

"I love black olives," Maggie said shyly, "but I like the others, too." Leo made a note of her preference, promising himself that he would get her favorite the next time. Suddenly he frowned. What the hell was this "next time" business?

All the children stopped talking at once, even the friends that had joined them.

"Mr. Coulter?" Brenda asked, speaking for all of them as they absorbed his ferocious look. "Is everything all right?"

He smiled at her formal use of his name, realizing it was used as a barrier, and the room took a collective sigh, visibly relaxing. His grin became wider with that knowledge, too.

"I was just thinking that I could have bought twenty pizzas for you little devils and it probably wouldn't have been enough."

The children giggled, all admitting that he was right; they could all eat at least two a piece. Two of Kings-

ley's friends stood slightly apart from the group, their
eyes wide as they watched their friend banter with the
huge man. Brenda could tell that Kingsley's worth had
increased twofold with Leo's appearance. She was
pleased for her son's sake, but that knowledge also irritated. It was something that she couldn't do for her
son, no matter how hard she tried. Only another man
could impress a boy child it seemed. . . .

"Brenda?" Leo's voice intruded on her thoughts and
she turned to him, frowning. "Do you have any paper
plates or should the kids use napkins?"

He was standing patiently next to the kitchen cabinets, his eyes searching hers as if looking for the answer to another question altogether.

"Napkins," she snapped as she walked to the pantry
and pulled out a cellophane wrapped package of them.
Setting the pile in the center of the table was the signal
for the children to dig in.

Maggie watched carefully as the younger ones tried
to reach into the boxes and pull the pieces apart. Finally she had to help. Her little hands worked at the
slices, her patience apparent as she managed to get the
pizza square in the center of each napkin so there would
be no drippy mess on the floor.

As each one got their piece, Brenda made sure they
sat down around the table, some sharing seats, others
bending over the table itself. Voices rose and fell,
promises and threats of anyone getting more than their
share filling the air.

Brenda's frown was still in place when she looked up
to be snagged by Leo's sharp hazel-eyed gaze. She stiffened. Did the man have to look so damn intimidating?

Her eyes flashed back the message and Leo's brows rose in haughty question. She could almost hear him saying, *What have I done that's eating at you?* She wanted to answer him aloud in the worst way, but the answer wasn't that simple. How could she explain that he had just scored points with the neighborhood children that she could never beat? How stupid that would sound, no matter how real the emotion was behind it!

"Pizza?" Leo asked her.

"No, thanks," she muttered. Without another word she walked out of the kitchen and into the hallway, not stopping until she was standing at the living room window, staring out through the tears that threatened.

"What is it?" Leo said behind her, placing his large hands gently on her shoulders.

She jumped at the sound of his voice. "Do you have to sneak up on people like that?"

His deep chuckle seemed to fill the room, "No one has ever accused me of being hard to see or hear before," he said.

"Well, I am. I came in here for a little peace and quiet. I didn't expect to be followed around my own home." Her voice was low with anger.

His brows rose again. "I thought I was a guest, not a shadow."

She turned on her heel to face him, her brown eyes sparking golden fire. Her long brown hair swung around her shoulders to catch the glint of sunlight breaking through the window. "A guest is usually invited. You barged in here like some tall Greek god and expected to bowl us over with your gifts!"

She could see the confusion in his face. "Pizza? This is a gift from the gods?" he asked incredulously.

"Yes!" she exclaimed heatedly. "Because you can afford it and I couldn't even begin to, it turns into a very *large* gift!"

His hazel eyes turned into green ice chips. "I'll send you the bill, lady," he said in a low, vibrating voice.

But she didn't heed the tone he used. "That's just it. If you sent me three bills, I couldn't pay for it! I couldn't buy the children the status symbol you just bought. I couldn't afford it! So now, because I've got to hold this family together, I'll look like the piker. But you! You come off looking like a hero to my children and their friends. You get all the glory!"

One large hand ran through his blond hair. "I don't believe this," he muttered, almost to himself. "You mean to tell me that this argument is because you're jealous that I could buy pizzas for the kids and you couldn't?"

"Yes!" she practically screamed, not listening to how childish her viewpoint sounded. "And after this morning, when you gave the biggest busybody on the block something to talk about for the next month, I think this move was very underhanded!"

Leo went rigid and fought to control his anger. "Lady," he said in a quiet but deadly tone. "You have got a problem. A big one. I've heard sick women before, but you take the cake."

Her temper hit flash point. How dare he call her mentally ill. "You don't know what sick is, mister." She took his arm and practically dragged him down the hallway to her bedroom. When they reached the doorway, though, he balked. "I'll show you what sick is."

She ran to the large closet door and flung it open. The closet was arranged with a minimum of dresses, skirts and blouses hanging neatly on the rod. Along one side were shelves from ceiling to floor. They were filled with labeled boxes holding wrappings from everything to canned vegetables to paper towels and even a few chocolate-milk mixes.

He didn't move; it took all his concentration to absorb what was before him and try to come up with a logical explanation.

"Look at this!" she practically shouted, oblivious to his thoughts. "This is what I have to do just to keep our heads above water so I can afford to stay in this house and keep clothing on the children's backs!"

"Save old wrappers?" he asked caustically, "What do you do? Weave them into wool?"

It took a full, slack-jawed minute for her to register the fact that he had no idea what she was showing him. "You jackass! You don't even understand," she gritted through her teeth. "These are called 'proof of purchase' and with them and a few coupons, I get rebate money in the mail. With the rebate money I buy the children's clothing, pay for car repairs, look after whatever expense comes in that has to be met. It takes hours a week to work on this, but it's the only way we can make it." She stood with her hands on her hips, her eyes still spitting fire at him.

"Doesn't your husband pay child support?" He thought the question was a reasonable one, so why was she looking at him as if he was now the crazy one?

"Do you think I'd have to do this if he did?" Her laugh was brittle. "My husband is considered unemployed. He's his new wife's lapdog. He hasn't got any money; she has it all. And they both like it that way. He even signed a prenuptial agreement to ensure that she wouldn't have to carry his debts. Isn't that wonderful? The man is just what she wanted, a spineless wonder who doesn't cost her anything but room and board. And in exchange he treats her as if she were a princess in a fairy tale." Her anger was still there, along with the frustration of her own problems. "Now do you understand why buying four pizzas is an expense that I can't afford, even if I wanted to?"

"Yes," he said as he watched her ire dissolve. "But whether or not a man holds a job, he still has to pay child support. You should sue him for it."

"With what? Proofs of purchase? It costs money to hire an attorney. Besides, if he paid he would probably think he had to see the children again, and I don't want that. They're used to his being gone, and I think we'd all be better off without the weekly hassle of his visits. This way I have the house and car and he has his freedom."

Her shoulders slumped and her head bowed. She looked like a droopy flower without enough energy to seek the sun, and his heart gave a squeeze as he began to realize just how much she had to fight to keep her family together and in some semblance of a unit.

He took the necessary steps across the room and enfolded her in his large arms, resting her head against his massive chest exactly where his heart was beating. One hand soothed her hair, the other held her close to him.

Without thinking of her response, she clasped her arms around his waist and burrowed her head between his chest and arm, feeling secure in his grasp. It felt good to be held again, to be close to a man and know the feel and scent of him....

"I'm sorry," he said quietly, letting her go gently. His hand came under her chin and lifted her face up to his. His lips brushed tantalizingly over hers, once, twice, teasing every nerve in her body.

Then he turned before she could utter another word. Within seconds he was out the front door and gone. His car engine came to life and he drew away from the curb.

Brenda wished fervently that Sam Lewis had never tried his matchmaking skills on her. But just the same, her arms crossed in front of her, hugging Leo's warmth to her body.

BRENDA SLIPPED THE FINISHED CONTRACT out of the word-processing printer, checked it over thoroughly, then set it aside to have a label made for the envelope. One more copy to print out and Monday's work would be done. Then she could wearily crawl into the car and head for home. Although her bout of flu had passed, thank goodness, she still felt as if she'd been run over by a freight train.

She rethreaded the fan-fold paper into the printer and flipped the necessary switches to make one more copy. After the printer began its staccato tapping, she lowered the lid on the soundproof cover and sat back. She rubbed her temples in a circular motion, trying to ease the tension before it blossomed into a knockout of a headache.

Sam's phone had not stopped ringing today. For that matter, neither had April's. Both partners, whether they wanted to be or not, were in big demand.

That also meant that she couldn't give him the full treatment of her temper, either. When she had walked in this morning, she'd been able to get across the fact that she was angry with him for not telling her about Leo's ticket, but that was as far as it got. The phones started ringing and the rest of the staff had come in with questions about the work load. For all Sam knew, she had accepted his hastily whispered apology—and that wasn't the case at all! She grinned. There would be plenty of time later to make him think twice about interfering with her life again. . . .

When the hallway door opened, Brenda automatically pasted a smile on her face in preparation for another client.

But the smile drooped considerably when she saw who it was. Think of the devil and he'll appear, a friend of hers used to say, and now she almost believed it. Only this one was a large, blond, handsome bear of a man. His dark gray suit was another custom-made one that underlined his masculinity, but what choice did he have with a build like that?

"Hello, Brenda." Leo's voice shot through her system, speeding her heartbeat to double time. His hazel-green eyes seemed to delve into her very flesh all the way through to her backbone.

"Hello, Mr. Coulter." She glanced down at the appointment book, grateful for the chance not to look at him. "Do you have an appointment with Mr. Lewis or have I overlooked something?" she asked, attempting to keep the distance between them by the tone of her voice and the use of Sam's proper title.

A faint smile tugged at his lips. "No appointment. I was passing by and dropped in to say hi."

"Oh?" She tried to keep a slightly cool, professional note in her voice. It was practically impossible, but she gave it her best shot, anyway. "If you'll give me a moment, I'll buzz as soon as he gets off the phone."

Leo's arms crossed his massive chest, tightening the sleeves of his well-cut suit to show off his perfectly formed biceps. "You misunderstand. I came by to say hi to you. Not to Sam."

Tact. Diplomacy. Reserve. Professionalism. They all deserted her at once. All she could do was frown, close her mouth and then open it again to ask a question. "Why, for heaven's sake?"

His eyes twinkled, his smile widened to warm her blood. "Obviously because I wanted to."

Tact was still missing from her repertoire. "But why? I'm not even a redhead!"

His brows slowly rose as he seemed to contemplate her observation, his gaze touching her hair, her eyes, her blushing cheeks. "No, you aren't, are you?" he asked as if just noticing it himself.

"And I don't have a willowy figure or long legs."

"Am I doomed to stay true to someone else's estimation of my character? Can't I deviate from form once in a while?"

"Not with me," she said, a firmness in her voice that seemed to surprise them both. "I'm not into surprises, nor am I about to be an experiment for broadening your tastes."

"I don't remember asking you to be either of those things," Leo said calmly, completely unruffled by Brenda's caustic comments. "I *am* asking that you don't attempt to fit me or my tastes in a small box and label them like you do envelopes."

Brenda's stiff back slowly relaxed. "I'm sorry, Mr. Coulter. That was unfair and I apologize." The words were jerky, but the apology was honest.

Once more his eyes twinkled with warmth. "Are you sorry enough to have a drink with me before you head for home?"

"No, I . . ." She couldn't think of a thing to say.

He unfolded his arms and leaned down toward her, his hands splaying on the desk top and the thin gold band of his watch catching the light. "You're not sorry, or you're not heading for home tonight?"

"Neither," she snapped. "No, both." Now she was confused. Taking a deep breath, she began again. "I'm going straight home tonight. And I am sorry. I'm afraid that my tongue runs away with me sometimes."

His smile took in the worry around her eyes. "Don't say no. I promise I'll be on my best behavior. Just one drink at the lounge around the corner from here."

Again she asked that direct question. "Why?"

He shrugged, his eyes drifting away from her. Standing straighter, he placed his hands in his pants' pockets, straining the material tautly across the front of his hips. "I really don't know. I just wanted to have a drink with you. No strings attached."

"Brenda!" Sam's voice bellowed from behind the closed door.

"Her master's voice," Brenda said dryly but with a bit of secret relief. Standing, she reached for her shorthand pad and pencil at the same time.

As she leaned over, the vee of her blouse billowed slightly. Leo got a delightful glance of soft, full breasts pressing against the binding of her cream-tinted bra. He couldn't seem to pull his eyes away from the luscious view. She straightened just in time to see the direction of his gaze and another blush tinted her apricot cheeks.

Sam's door burst open and he walked into the general office area, a sheaf of papers in his hand. "Brenda, I..." he began before he saw Leo standing across from her desk. "Leo!" he exclaimed, a smile lighting his face. "What the hell are you doing here? Slumming?" he teased as they shook hands.

"Trying to talk your secretary into having a drink with me," Leo admitted, his eyes twinkling as they grazed Brenda before returning to Sam.

A full thirty seconds passed before Sam spoke. A myriad of expressions flitted across his face, with an answering expression from Leo. They seemed to silently communicate whole paragraphs that Brenda couldn't hear. She had a feeling that it concerned her, and it made her uncomfortable. She fidgeted with her pencil, placing the tip in the wire binding of her steno pad.

"Well," Sam drawled slowly, his eyes darting from Brenda's unconsciously nervous gesture to Leo. "And she's already told you no, hasn't she? Our Brenda hasn't got a fun bone in her body unless she's laughing at the boss, that is. You should have asked me—I would have saved you the embarrassment of a refusal."

Brenda's head shot up, her eyes sparkling, ready for battle. How dare Sam say that about her! He might also be her good friend, but he needn't embarrass her.

Without even putting her thoughts in order, Brenda straightened and turned toward Leo. "Mr. Coulter, I would love to have one drink with you. But I have to leave by six-thirty to relieve my baby-sitter."

As soon as she said the words she was shocked. Her only sense of satisfaction came from the fact that both men were as stunned as she was. Her eyes narrowed in anger at Sam. No, only Leo was stunned. Sam was as smug and complacent as a mouse with his own cheese factory. He had said that on purpose to bait her! And because she had jumped at it, it had worked.

She muttered an unladylike expletive under her breath, her eyes darting arrows at her boss.

Before Sam could say anything more, Leo chuckled. "Thanks, Brenda. How much more do you have to do here before you're finished?"

Her steno pad smacked against the desk top, the pencil following. Stupid female! "I'll be ready in fifteen minutes," she said through gritted teeth. She might go, but she sure as heck wasn't going to have fun or entertain Mr. Leo Coulter with a sparkling personality! This was his idea; he could suffer the consequences. He had nerve asking her, anyway. Didn't he know when someone didn't care for him? Was he totally insensitive or just dumb?

Sam ushered Leo into his office. "While Brenda's finishing up, come talk to me about the Henderson case," he said as he closed the door behind him, leaving Brenda to her own anger.

She typed out a label, turned off the computer and printer, stuffed the envelope with the newly printed contracts and set it aside for the messenger service that would pick it up in the morning. With her desk straightened and a glance at tomorrow's appointments, she was finished for the day.

Now what?

Should she interrupt Leo and Sam to tell them that she was ready? Or should she just wait, hoping they'd talk until it was too late for her to go?

She reached for her jacket and purse. Or should she just leave and forget the whole embarrassing incident? That idea appealed to her the most. They would both get the message by her just not being there. When they finally ended their conversation and walked out, she'd be gone, giving them the snub they both deserved for putting her in this spot to begin with. She smiled. Perfect. Perhaps then Sam would drop this ridiculous obsession he had about her dating.

It wasn't until her hand was on the knob and she was opening the outer door that they walked in. Leo stopped in his tracks, his eyes narrowing as he pointedly glanced from her face to her hand on the door, then back again. "Ready?" he asked in a deceptively casual tone.

Her face felt like the hot sun. Her hand dropped away from the door to clench at her purse. With a determined tilt to her small chin, she nodded her head.

In two steps he was at her side, his large hand holding the door open for her to pass through. She hesitated only a moment, her mind not working as well as it should. But her senses were. They felt his presence next to her, smelled the scent of him, saw the overpowering handsomeness of his blond hair, green eyes and strong build. She even heard his light breath turn into a small, intimate chuckle.

"Night, Brenda," Sam said from the door of his office, his face lit with a smile. His eyes, however, showed just a tinge of concern.

"Night, Sam," she said with a croak in her throat. Then she walked through the door as regally as a queen on her way to execution. An example for us all . . .

They said nothing as they waited for the elevator. The ride down was also quiet. The walk to Leo's car was carried out in silence. Finally Brenda couldn't take it anymore.

"Did you have a nice day?" she asked cheerfully, mentally hitting herself for such a dumb, stupid remark!

"A very nice day," he answered blandly, slipping her into the passenger seat. "Did you?"

Before she could answer, he had closed her door and was walking around the front of the car to reach the driver's side.

When he slipped in, she answered, "It was very hectic."

He placed the key in the ignition and started the car. "Have you ever thought of doing something else?" he asked as he pulled into the flow of traffic.

"Of course. I'm the perfect homemaker. Unfortunately, I'm not the perfect wife, so that career's not open to me." Her voice was laced with bitterness, her hands clenched on her lap. This was going to be one long hour!

"Why? Have you tried being a housewife more than once?"

She looked at him with her wide brown eyes. Was he crazy? "No. Once was enough."

"But if you didn't like your job as a secretary, wouldn't you try another office?" She was right. He was crazy!

"Finding another job and marrying another man are two different barrels of pickles, Mr. Coulter."

"Leo," he inserted absently. "And I don't see the difference. They're both careers."

"You must have a terrific time in court," she muttered, more to herself than to him. But her comment earned her a smile that warmed up the entire interior of the car.

"You think I'm crazy, don't you?" he said with a chuckle in his voice. He must be crazy, talking about the one subject that he had always considered closed: marriage.

"In a word?" Her voice was dry. "Yes."

This time the chuckle spilled out to reverberate through the car and into Brenda's body, filling her with a warmth she hadn't felt in years. She couldn't help but join in the laughter. He pulled into the parking lot of the bar and grill, slipping the car into an empty slot. Within two minutes they were out of the car and inside the lounge.

It was filled with commuters stopping off on their way home from offices in the vicinity. The decor was dark, with wood-toned walls. It was a friendly place where apparently most of the customers knew or at least were acquainted with one another.

Leo took her arm, leading her toward the back booth where a small Reserved sign sat on the table.

"This is someone else's table," she murmured.

"I know," he said as he took the sign and tossed it toward the salt and pepper shakers that hugged the booth wall. "Now it's ours." After making sure she was seated, he sat across from her, his hazel-green eyes staring at her as if she were a very special bug under his very own microscope.

An impish grin lit her face, teasing him with the hint of dimples that sat just below the corners of her eyes. Why hadn't he noticed them before?

"Well?" she asked. "Which am I?"

"What?"

"Am I a bacteria or a virus?"

Ruefully he smiled. "Was I being so obvious?"

"Yes," she said honestly. Whether she wanted to be or not, she was here. She might as well be herself and enjoy it.

"I was thinking that you're a very intricate female, Ms Hunt," he said equally honest. Honest enough to know that he couldn't call her Mrs. without conjuring up pictures of her with another man. And that didn't sit well with him. But he wasn't masochistic enough to delve into the reasons why he felt that way.

"Oh, how's that?"

"Because you have so many facets. You're a great secretary or Sam wouldn't rely on you the way he does. You're a great mother if those cute little Indians are anything to go by. And you're one hell of a home-maker if you can get enough money on rebates to help pay for the little extras in life." He leaned back, his suit jacket opened to expose the matching vest underneath. The dark gray of the material hugged his body, as did the white silk shirt under it.

It was funny that the more he relaxed, the more tense she became. It seemed to be a tug-of-war as to who was in control, making whomever it was relaxed while the other felt hunted.

If she wanted to relax, then she'd better get back into control again. "Thank you for the lavish compliments. Is there a method to your madness, or do you just feel like generously littering the air with beautiful phrases tonight?"

The waitress came, took their order and left. Leo was still relaxed. With sudden insight, Brenda realized what the waitress had known all along. "My God, you really did reserve this table!" she muttered in disbelief.

"I thought I told you that." he said calmly.

"You did, but I didn't believe you. Who ever heard of a man reserving a booth in a bar and grill, anyway?"

"I would have reserved a table in the best restaurant, but I had this funny idea that you wouldn't join me," he said as the waitress quickly appeared with their drinks.

She sipped at the glass of white wine the waitress brought, unable to look at him. "You're probably right."

"Why?" he asked in a low voice that she could still hear over the dull roar of the other customers. "Do I scare you? Or are you just not interested in getting to know me?"

"No, I—" She stopped, glancing up to see the earnestness in his expression. He wasn't being coy or fishing for compliments. He honestly wanted to know. She smiled ruefully. "Yes, you frighten me," she said slowly. "For some reason you tend to get my back up and I automatically want to fight you."

"Why?"

She shrugged, her smile now drooping. "I don't know."

A heavy sigh passed his lips. One large hand combed his hair back from its favorite resting place on his forehead, only to have it spill forward again. But when he looked up and smiled, the entire room seemed to be filled with a golden light. The golden man, she thought before chiding herself for being romantic enough to wax lyrical. She decided to place both feet back on the ground before he made her forget more than she should. "Besides, I don't date much, as you know. Aside from not being able to afford the baby-sitting fees, I have three 'Indians' at home that need constant care."

"Isn't it customary for the male to pick up the baby-sitting costs? If he asks her out, then it's his responsibility." He noted the sudden change in her. She'd definitely stiffened, had sat up straighter. But why?

"Maybe in your circle of friends, but not in mine," she said with such determination that he knew there was no way to persuade her otherwise.

"Brenda, I'd like to see you again. I think we could become friends and I'd like that," he said haltingly, his hand now holding the stein of beer as if it were made of uncrushable metal. He let go of his drink, reaching over to grasp her hand, which was on the table. His fingers were strong, slightly callused and warm, and damp in spots where the moisture of his drink had rubbed off. He turned her hand over, stroking the palm with his thumb.

She wanted to pull away, yet she couldn't. "I can't see how..." she began slowly, her mind whirling with thoughts she hadn't had in years. Not since she dated in high school.

"What about like we're doing tonight? Having a few drinks, enjoying each other's company in the midst of a crowd? You're protected by them, and I get to enjoy unwinding in your company." He let go of her hand and leaned back, showing her by his action just how harmless he was supposed to be.

Her eyes twinkled, a smile lit up her face, and once more she showed him the secret dimples at the corners of her eyes. "One drink, not a few," she corrected with a chuckle. "And yes, I'd like that, as long as you understand that I have to get home early."

"I understand," he said softly. He lifted his mug and tapped her wineglass. "Here's to unwinding," he said solemnly.

"To unwinding," she repeated, her voice almost as low as his. She raised her glass to her lips.

He fleetingly wondered if her definition of the word was the same as his. He wished it was, even though he knew better. This was going to be an interesting relationship.

BY SIX-THIRTY Brenda was home and fixing dinner. By seven she was cleaning the kitchen while Maggie and Janie sat at the kitchen table doing their homework. Kingsley considered himself adult enough to do his homework away from his mother's watchful eye. He now did it in his room, with the door open so Brenda could check if she wanted.

By nine-thirty the children were in bed and Brenda sat on the couch by herself, attempting to sew another hem into Janie's dress. She was going to have to tack lace where the old hemline was so that the white crease line wouldn't show.

How many nights had she sat and worked on the children's clothing, trying to make it stretch for one more wear, week or month? Forever, it seemed.

Only this evening, she didn't seem to mind. In fact she even found herself humming a tune she had heard earlier. One that Catherine Sinclair—Lewis—had made popular recently. It was from a remake of *Oklahoma* that was due to be released next month. Brenda smiled. Catherine and Sam should be parents about the same time the movie premiered.

Although still withholding some small part of her judgment, she had to admit that Catherine had been good for Sam. He was so much more relaxed, happy with himself and his life since he met her. It was as if he had found what everyone else searched for in life. Even Catherine was different than Brenda had imagined, warmer and more easygoing than she had expected the singer to be.

She had never seen two people so much in love, unless it was April and Jace. And lately she'd never seen them so harried. April had had triplets, all boys, eight weeks ago. They were carbon copies of Jace but with April's happy smile. Because she now had capable help—an entire household of help, come to think of it— she had just returned to work twice a week. The rest of the time she spent with her brand-new family. She and Jace were constantly complaining, but the ecstatic glint in their eyes belied their words.

Brenda leaned back, her eyes staring unseeing out the living room window. She had been so jealous when Sam had been married. Oh, not because she had wanted him for herself, because she hadn't, not as a lover. But he was such a wonderful, caring man that she hadn't wanted to see him get hurt. And—she had to face it—she had been jealous of Catherine and her successful career and life. She had everything, while Brenda barely made it from paycheck to paycheck.

Sometimes it seemed that everyone had a better time of it than she did. Until she looked at the children. Her children were her life force, and underneath all the petty day-to-day things that went with just plain living, she knew it. Without them she would be lost, worthless and so very, very lonely. In fact, she had to admit in dark moments that they might be the only thing between herself and pure unadulterated bitterness with life. If only David . . .

That thought brought a complete halt to all other thoughts. Was that what was the matter with her? Had she lived with a bitterness over her divorce that spilled into others' lives. Was that what Sam kept hinting at? What Leo Coulter thought of her? Was that why Catherine and April had been so sweet, trying to make her see that everyone had something in their past they would rather forget, but that they shouldn't let it color their future? Had she turned into one of those bitter, dried-up women who cried about their plight in life, but refused to accept anything new or different?

Brenda sat up straight, her hands covering her stomach as if she had just been punched. She remembered the rude, bossy way she had treated Leo at the Music

Hall and flinched. Then the way he had looked when she had been trying to sneak out of the office this afternoon: hurt and somehow very sad. It was his sadness that had made her feel guilty. All he had done was ask her out for a drink and she had treated him as if he had leprosy, instead of agreeing immediately because that's what she had secretly wanted to do all along. But over the years she had gotten into the habit of denying herself any fun because the thought of having fun was more scary than staying home and crying about her plight in life.

"My God!" she said aloud. "I've turned into exactly what I've always hated in others. A bitter, whining, middle-aged woman who'll do nothing except get worse as she gets older."

Her voice echoed in the room to bounce back on her own ears as if to confirm her words.

But what could she do about it? She had no money, no choice in life-style.

"You could change your outlook, you simpleton," she muttered as an answer, and surprised herself by agreeing. Then came the next question. "But how?"

As if she had always known the answer, it came to her. She might not be able to change the circumstances of her life, but she could certainly change herself.

She'd begin by taking the first step, then after that one step at a time.

5

"FLYNN-SULLIVAN, LEWIS, ATTORNEYS," Brenda said in her best business voice. The girl who usually answered the phone and forwarded the calls to their respective desks was already gone for the day.

"Can you meet me for drinks tonight?" Leo's voice came over the wires to tingle down her spine. They hadn't seen each other in a week.

"Who are you asking, me or the receptionist?" Brenda teased.

"You. I'd know your voice anywhere," he said quietly. "Can you?"

"Yes," she answered, her breath catching in her throat.

"Same time?"

"Yes," she said almost in a whisper.

"Good," he replied briskly, as if someone had just stepped into his office. "I'll see you then."

She couldn't help teasing him, knowing there was little he could do about it. "Have you reserved our booth or should I check out the bar first?"

"The former. It had better not be the latter." He made it clear that he was eager to be with her.

"Yes, sir," she said with a chuckle, suddenly feeling as if sunshine had filtered through to the inner office.

She glanced down at her dress, a coffee-colored cotton that was one of her best. It looked crisp yet sophisticated. One of her neighbors had made it for her in exchange for Brenda watching her children while she and her husband had gone away for a long weekend. Long live the barter system....

She completed her work quickly, glad that this wasn't April's day in the office. Occasionally her secretary would ask Brenda to help with last-minute details since April did enough work for the entire week when she was in the office only two or three days.

Waving a silent goodbye to Sam, who was on the phone, she was out the door in a flash, her stomach telling her that she had a large case of butterflies. It had been exactly one week since she'd seen Leo. He had called several times, both at home and at the office, but neither had been able to synchronize their schedules with the other.

Would he notice any difference in her? She had changed her makeup slightly, bringing it more up-to-date. At her mirror's suggestion, she had begun to wear her hair down again, allowing it to curl around her shoulders and softly frame her face. It made her look years younger and less heavy.

She had also started jogging in the evening when the children were doing their homework. At first she could hardly make it the length of her small block, but after a week, she was doing much better. She was going to lose the seven pounds she had always sworn that she would lose someday. Someday was now.

But the big change was in her attitude. Whenever Leo called she made an effort to be nice rather than snap at every little thing he said. It wasn't as if he was being romantic and she was fending off advances. Quite the reverse. He seemed to want to talk to her as a friend, discuss the day, talk about the kids. At first Brenda thought he was prying, then she realized he was really interested and began, slowly, to tell him about the children. It felt good to discuss them with someone who was interested.

She finally reached the bar, slightly breathless and high on the anticipation of seeing Leo again, although she wouldn't admit it.

She walked into the dimly lit lounge they had first had drinks in, standing still to give her eyes time to adjust. Then she saw him. He was at the end of the bar, two drinks in his hand as a woman smiled up at him, her hand gently tugging on his lapel. Brenda's heart did a flip-flop, settling somewhere down near her toes.

He smiled at the woman, then gave one of those delicious chuckles of his. The sound cruised through Brenda's entire nervous system. If she could have, she would have fled, but her feet seemed to be anchored to the floor. Certainly her eyes were riveted to him!

Leo glanced up just in time to see her. She stood at the other end of the bar, one hand holding on to a small dark purse, while her other hand clutched at the rounded corner of the bar. Her face was white, her mouth slightly open in a pouted O her coffee-brown eyes larger than he had ever seen.

His eyes narrowed, his smile disappearing. He wasn't sure what to do—call her to him or go to her. His instincts told him that if he made a move toward her, she'd run away.

He raised both glasses toward her, once more smiling, hoping he was sending the right message and that she'd see and understand.

"Who's that?" the other woman asked in petulant voice.

"My wife," he answered, knowing that this woman would now drop her come-on. She had begun a conversation with him when he had stepped up to the bar to order drinks. Just another woman, not worth the time of day. He backed away from her and slowly edged his way toward "their" booth, hoping—no, fervently praying—that Brenda would follow.

Brenda stood stiffly, debating the situation. She wanted to join him more than anything in the world, but she couldn't help wondering if he was always entertaining himself with someone else the minute she wasn't around.

What was she thinking of. He wasn't her husband, her lover or even her boyfriend! He was just a friend she was meeting for a casual drink. Nothing more. There were no strings in their relationship. There never had been.

What right did she have to demand them now?

"Hi, honey. Waiting for someone or can I buy you a drink?" A dark-haired young man came from behind her, putting his arm around her waist. She never gave him a second glance, nor bothered to shrug off his hand.

She watched Leo move slowly between the tables toward the booth. "Waiting for someone," she muttered, not even realizing what she was saying.

"Who, honey?" the guy said. "Maybe I can keep you company until they come."

"My husband. And he's here," she said coldly, finally turning to stare at the man until his arm dropped from her waist. "Excuse me."

Leo reached the table and placed a drink on each side. He was almost afraid to turn around in case Brenda had gone. His palms itched to close around something, anything, and squeeze it. Preferably that floozy at the bar who had caused all this. Finally, when he couldn't stand it anymore, he turned.

He finally took a breath, not realizing until that moment that he had been holding it.

She was still there.

She had just shrugged off some charmer's hand and was coming toward him. He had never felt so angry and so relieved at the same time. If looks could kill, he would have maimed the other man in several places, a few more painful than others. Then his whole line of vision was taken with Brenda. He watched her walk toward him, gracefully weaving her way through the tables. He smiled at her, relief plainly shining in his eyes. When she smiled back, his shoulders loosened from their stiffly held position.

"Hi," he said softly as she stepped to his side. He stared down into her brown eyes, losing himself in the depth of them.

"Hi, yourself," she answered huskily. "I didn't know if you were busy or just caught in a cute situation."

"A cute situation." He couldn't keep his hand at his side. It came up and tilted her chin so that he could graze his lips against hers. "It wasn't of my making. I figured I'd get our drinks now, so we could talk longer."

"I figured as much," she said, her lips still slightly parted as if asking for another kiss. He brushed her lips again, wishing that he and Brenda were somewhere else. Anywhere but here. Somewhere that he could take her in his arms and tenderly hold her small frame against his larger one until he was really sure that she was here, with him.

"You're beautiful," he murmured, surprising both himself and Brenda by his admission. "You are," he underlined his original statement by repeating it.

Brenda hesitated only a second. The old Brenda would have hotly denied it, then accused him of wanting something. But the new Brenda was here now. "Thank you," she said simply.

"You're welcome," he teased, his green eyes lighting with an inner merriment. "What about you?"

"What?" She looked confused, her eyes slightly out of focus as his thumb stopped to caress the center of her bottom lip.

"Was that guy keeping you busy or was it just a cute situation?"

She grinned. "I was his good deed for the day. He was trying to make an old lady feel good by giving her his thirty-second pass."

He dropped his hand from her throat and helped her into the booth. His hand felt cold without touching her flesh. "Thirty-second pass, hell," he muttered, sitting across from her. "There's no such thing unless he had a football in his hand."

Brenda's skin turned a beautiful apricot as she remembered what she had told the young man. "He was just being friendly."

Leo grunted, his irritation still apparent.

It was time to change the subject, although she had to admit to herself that she liked Leo's display of jealousy. Whether it was real or faked, it felt good.

"How was the concert Saturday?"

Leo's brows almost disappeared into his blond hair. "How'd you know I went?"

"You were with Sam and Catherine, remember?" She smiled, but it didn't quite reach her eyes. She also knew that he had taken a luscious redhead with him.

"It was nice," he answered just before almost completely downing the beer. His eyes looked everywhere but at her.

"Do you enjoy concerts?" she asked casually, sipping on her white wine. It tasted like gasoline.

"Not particularly," Leo said honestly. "Do you?"

She smiled. "Not particularly. I like operas more. I can see the action. I like more than one sense to be stimulated."

Now it was his turn to smile, and the smile turned into a low, velvety chuckle. "So do I, Brenda. So do I."

If he had said that last week, she would have probably been offended right down to her toes. But she couldn't help it—he was such an endearing flirt—she couldn't keep the giggles inside.

Leo leaned back, delighting in the sound. His eyes, his relaxed position, everything told her that he enjoyed being with her.

In turn, she leaned back and relaxed.

"Care for another, Mrs. Coulter? Mr. Coulter?" The waitress stood at their table, a polite smile on her lips.

"Oh," Brenda began, wondering how she would explain to him what she had said.

But Leo cut her off. "I'll have another. What about you, Brenda?" he asked, noticing that her face was as flushed as his. He couldn't very well explain the situation now, not after he had told the woman at the bar that Brenda was his wife. The waitress must have overheard him. He only hoped that Brenda would think it was a natural slip.

"Please," she said, then her mouth clamped shut. She knew that they would know Leo's name from his charge card. But the waitress must have overheard her at the bar with that young man. How could she explain that to Leo? She couldn't. Better to be quiet than to cause a scene. Especially with Leo.

She smiled at the wall, pretending that no one was near her. She'd rather slip through the floor than let Leo know she had claimed him as her husband. Husband! He'd bolt immediately in the other direction. Any direction except hers!

"Everything all right?" Leo's voice intruded on her thoughts. He put his hand over hers. His thumb once again rubbed her palm. "I'm sorry about the mistake. It's a natural one, though."

"I know," she replied, her voice barely above a whisper, her eyes watching their entwined hands. His touch was driving everything out of her mind.

"Tell me about the kids," he said, changing the subject. Anything so that she'd look at him again. "Is Janie doing better in school?"

"No, she's just learning to bat her eyelashes faster," Brenda said with a chuckle, relaxing once more. "Sometimes I worry about her turning into a regular Mata Hari, her skill is so well developed."

"Maybe it's because she has Maggie to be sensible and Kingsley to be commanding," Leo remarked quietly. "She's learned to develop a talent that neither of them can compete with as readily."

Brenda stared at her drink for a moment before looking up. "You know, that could be it," she said slowly, her eyes widening with the truth of the thought.

Leo sipped his beer. "Just an idea," he replied, shrugging his shoulders.

"It's more than that. You've met my children twice and yet you've pegged them exactly. How did you do that?" If she hadn't known better, she would have sworn he had blushed.

"I had a younger brother who did everything I didn't. And anything that I did well, he'd stay away from. Sibling rivalry comes in all forms," he said almost shyly.

"Were you close in age?"

"We weren't close in any way." For a moment Leo's eyes grew distant. "He was just a kid when our parents died. When I became the head of the house, he resented me as he would have resented my parents, only worse." He took another gulp of his beer, then stared down at the table as if talking to it. "The most peace either of us ever had was the first day we parted to live alone." His voice was hesitant, his thoughts faraway.

Her mouth formed a small circle as she recognized the hurt that had just surfaced. But now wasn't the time to delve. He felt too uncomfortable talking about his family, and she suddenly wanted to put him at ease.

He looked up, a sad smile on his face. "Tell me what the kids have been up to," he prompted.

She continued with the stories, content to bask in his interest. Occasionally Leo tossed out an idea or two, and she would respond, again surprised that he had such an insight into children.

The time went by too quickly. It seemed as if they had just begun to talk when Leo reminded her that it was time to leave.

He walked her to her car, promising himself that soon, very soon, he was going to make love to her or melt on the sidewalk trying. He couldn't take too much more of this waiting game.

Then perhaps he could get on with his life, and Brenda wouldn't intrude on his thoughts constantly.

Yes, he wanted to take her to bed and make love to her in one hundred and one ways. After he had done that, he was sure that she would be out of his mind and his system, and then he would be able to continue his bachelor existence without damage.

Besides, it would be good for both of them. A little exercise to relieve some of this pent-up frustration.

He was sure that, just like with the other women in his life, once he had her, the excitement would dwindle until he couldn't wait to get away from her. It was the cure-all for all his relationships.

He had just never had to wait so long to fulfill his own erotic fantasies. And these were definitely fantasies. He hadn't had such active ones since he'd been a teenager in high school who believed that anything that felt this good should be indulged in constantly!

BRENDA SAT UP IN BED, a book in her hand. She had been reading the same sentence over and over again. Her mind was replaying the early evening with Leo.

He was so handsome! His huge build and blond hair and hazel eyes were a combination that could hardly be beat. And she had the feeling that he knew it, only it didn't seem to be all-consuming with him as it was with some other men. He didn't trade on his good looks.

But it was his wonderful sense of humor that she loved the most. He found laughter in the most unusual places. And it was contagious. She had never felt so lighthearted and free as she had when she was with him.

Brenda would always be grateful for his patience with her, even after they stopped seeing each other, which she was sure would happen. He had shown her that she needed to get out and find a new perspective. And she had. Just the two early evenings they'd shared had made her realize that she should have begun dating again rather than hiding from life while lamenting its passing.

She owed Leo a lot.

She put the book on the nightstand, finally giving up. After turning out the light, Brenda curled around the extra pillow and closed her eyes.

But sleep didn't come. Although she had put in a full day, cooked dinner and cleaned dishes, then jogged around the block, her mind wasn't sleepy. It conjured up visions of Leo, naked, leaning over her, stroking her hands, her feet, her stomach, her legs, her breasts. He was a golden mountain of a man who would take her on a voyage of love to places she had never seen.

Stop it, she chided herself.

Erotic dreams were a waste of time. She didn't get paid for them, but she did get paid for being in the office, alert and ready for a full day's work.

Her last thought as sleep softly covered her brain with a blanket was that Leo was probably out with one of his redheads right now. No man like Leo Coulter would be satisfied with seeing a woman for drinks, then going home to sit in front of the TV. Not when he could have any woman he wanted.

She ignored the deflated feeling that gave her, promising herself that she was only looking for an occasional evening with him while she worked at bringing herself out of her shell and back into the world of the living.

THE FOLLOWING AFTERNOON Leo leaned back in his leather desk chair, running a hand around his neck in an attempt to release the tension in his muscles. It had been a hell of a day. He propped the telephone back on his shoulder and began scribbling on the pad in front of him. "I understand the complications, Kurt, and even though this is out of my realm, I know someone who can help you. His name's Sam Lewis and he's a corporate attorney. Give him a call and he'll set you and Victoria up so you can live in Europe and still maintain a tight control on your money and taxes."

He listened, then made a few more notes. "Right. *Newstime* magazine needs its own help in that area, but if your family is moving to Europe so Victoria can write and you can play in the sand, don't expect me to feel sorry for you." Leo chuckled. "And give Victoria a kiss for me. Tell her I read her last historical romance and it was great."

A moment later he ended the conversation and hung up the phone.

Closing his eyes, he tried to clear his mind of the day's business. But he didn't quite succeed.

Was everyone happily married lately, or was he just noticing it? The divorce rate was supposed to be up. Didn't people know that? Kurt and Victoria Morgan, Sam and Catherine, Jace and April: they were all acting as if their marriages would last forever.

"Bah," Leo said under his breath. "Humbug."

It made him feel better to say it aloud, but he certainly felt foolish lying to the only person who knew him best . . . himself.

The fact was that marriage was alive and well. It just wasn't for him. He was more the love-'em-and-leave-'em type. But if he ran across a divorcée and her brood and enjoyed them for a short time in his life, what was wrong with that? It didn't mean that he had to empty her closets of "proof of purchases" and move in, did it? Of course not. It only meant that he had to figure out a way to lower her guard to get her into bed before he went crazy, or blind or died trying.

He stood up, no longer tired.

He'd start tonight. He'd cook dinner for her at her place, show her that he was a nice guy, relax and enjoy her company.

Then, when the little ones went to bed, he'd begin a very persuasive campaign to get her to tuck him into bed, too. Her bed.

He didn't want to delve any further into his own psyche and determine why he was so enthralled with a shorter browner version of womanhood. He didn't even want to know why he—a confirmed bachelor—liked the idea of her family so much. It was enough that he just . . . wanted.

WHEN BRENDA PULLED INTO THE DRIVEWAY, all the lights in the house were on.

When she reached the front door, she could hear the TV blaring. What were the kids doing home before she was? True the baby-sitter was her next-door neighbor, but they weren't supposed to go into the house without her there.

"Kingsley? Maggie? Is everything all right?" she asked as she unlocked and opened the front door.

All three children were sprawled on their stomachs, eyes glued to the screen as they watched a situation comedy. Without turning around, Kingsley answered. "Yeah, Mom, everything's fine. Mr. Coulter came by and we saw his car from Mrs. Konig's house, so we came home with him."

"Mr. Coulter?" Brenda's heart skipped a beat.

"Yes, he's in the kitchen."

Her heart pounded against her ribs. She quickly arranged her hair, making sure that the wind hadn't blown it into a mess, then she smoothed her skirt over her hips.

By the time she reached the kitchen doorway, she thought she had herself under control. After all, she was allowed to be a little nervous; she hadn't expected company—any company—when she arrived home.

Leo was standing over the stove, a wooden spoon in his hand as he stirred something in a very large pot. From the odor wafting through the air, Brenda would guess spaghetti sauce. One of her hand towels was tucked into the front of his dark brown slacks, not big enough to go around his waist.

"Hello. And what is the occasion?" she asked calmly, hoping he couldn't see her nervousness. He was so large, he seemed to dwarf her kitchen.

He turned, his eyes scouting her up and down as a slow building smile turned his sensuous mouth upward. "Hello, yourself. How was your day?"

"Tiring. Working for attorneys has got to be one of the all time 'award winning' jobs."

"Who gets the award, you or the attorney?" he teased softly, laying down the spoon and practically stalking across the room to stand in front of her.

"I do. You guys don't deserve a thing, including your wonderful secretaries." Her voice dwindled the closer he came. He seemed to loom over her.

"You're right. And this attorney is going to give this secretary a welcome-home kiss, because she works so hard and so long in a thankless job...." Leo's hands caressed both sides of her face before he bent down and kissed her. His touch was soft but firm, molding her body toward his. His arms came around and her flesh tensed as his hands trailed down her spine and around her ribs to her stomach. Nerves fluttered everywhere, shocking her out of her apathy. She felt as if she were almost flying. His tongue provocatively outlined the rim of her lips before he plunged in to taste the hidden sweetness there.

Without even realizing it, her arms went around him, and she used the strength of his large frame as an anchor. She couldn't think, couldn't even pull away. It was like nothing she had ever experienced before. His lips made magic on hers, turning her into a bundle of need.

Finally he pulled away. His forehead touched hers as they both caught their breath. "Oh, boy," he muttered, as if he was in trouble.

"You can say that again," she answered shakily.

"It's just a chemical reaction. A very *strong* chemical reaction."

"Yes," she agreed, fervently hoping he was right. For a moment she had thought it was an earthquake. "Tell me something," she said as she watched her hands run up and down his arms as if they belonged to someone else. It was time to change the subject. "Why are you an attorney? Why aren't you a football player or a bodyguard or a soldier, or something else?" Her lashes fluttered up to expose the soft brown of her eyes as they were caught by his.

He grinned self-consciously. "I never could play football. I had weak knees."

"Really? They look like tree trunks," she murmured, her voice almost a whisper.

His look was laced with satisfaction. "You noticed."

"Yes."

He grinned. "I'll tell you about my battle with sports sometime," he said, matching her whisper with his own ragged, deep voice.

"Promise?" She watched the way his lips moved, fascinated with the soft curve of them.

He smiled as he saw her eyes dilate with the same need that his body stirred with. "Promise," he repeated.

"You're very well built." Her voice was velvet moving over the most intimate parts of his body and making them respond instantaneously.

"Thank you. So are you." His lips touched her forehead and she closed her eyes with the wonder of his chaste kiss. It echoed through her body all the way down to her toes.

"I'll bet the girls were after you all the time."

"Looking back, they probably were," he said, chuckling. "But I was too into sports to notice. I was a virgin until my senior year when I turned seventeen. All the other guys were ahead of me."

"Perhaps not, they just had larger imaginations and bigger mouths."

"Think so?" His voice was definitely a whisper now. "Were you a virgin then?"

She smiled, opening her eyes to let him see the humor lurking there. "We all were at one time, Leo," she said trying to keep a straight face but not quite succeeding. "It's a temporary state at best. When it's gone, one wonders what all the fuss was about in the first place."

He chuckled again, his hands tightening on her back to draw her closer to his body, letting her feel what her nearness did to him. "Not me. I knew what the fuss was about and decided then and there that anything that could make me feel that good should be further explored."

Brenda tilted her head to the side, giving him a wide-eyed stare. "That good, huh?"

"Uh-huh. Terrific. It wasn't until I was into my twenties that I leaned to be discriminating in my choice of partners."

The softness left her eyes, her neck stiffened. "At least you learned," she said flatly. She tried to pull away, but his grip wouldn't lessen.

"Brenda, look at me," he urged. When she did, he sought the depth of her with his hazel-green gaze. "Does it make it any better to know that we all have someone in our life who has given us pain?"

Her brow furrowed. "You?"

He nodded his head. "Me."

"When?"

"When I was married to a little gal who said she couldn't stand the thought of being part of a military base for the rest of her life. Especially with just one man. She was working on the battalion when we parted." His eyes showed that there was far more to the story, but he tried to hide it by closing his lids and breathing in Brenda's scent.

Her eyes darkened with compassion. Her lips parted in a silent cry of pain as she realized just how much he must have suffered. At least David had not fooled around a lot. He had found one and then left. "It must have been awful."

"It was. It isn't anymore."

"Poor Leo," she said, her hand grazing the side of his jaw, feathering across his neck, then sweeping up to feel the thickness of his hair just behind his ear.

"Yes," he muttered, his brain buzzing with the nearness of her. "Poor Leo. Leo needs someone to comfort him, too."

Before she could answer, his lips had claimed hers, and he was molding to her as if she were putty, and she loved it. She melted against his flat stomach, taut thighs, her heart thudding against her rib cage so loudly that she was sure the sound reverberated in the air.

6

WHEN LEO PULLED AWAY, Brenda gave a small protesting moan. She wasn't ready to relinquish him so soon.

"Are you hungry?" he asked, swallowing the lump in his throat. He got it every time he looked down at the woman in his arms. He wanted to absorb her into himself, carry her with him so he could protect her from all the world and its hurts.

She smiled, keeping her eyes closed. Her head rested on his chest, listening to the beat of his heart, which sounded as erratic as hers. "Mmm," she murmured.

"For what? Me or spaghetti?"

Without even thinking, Brenda responded, "Both, and in that order."

"Thank God," he growled under his breath. She had finally acknowledged the powerful chemistry between them. Finally! And none too soon, either. Just moments before he fell apart with the need for her.

"When are we eating? What are you doing to Mommy, Mr. Coulter?" Janie stood just behind Brenda, her eyes wide with concern.

Brenda guiltily pulled out of Leo's arms and turned to her daughter. "I was giving him a hug, sweetheart, just like I give you when you do something very nice," she explained in a rather shaky voice.

Leo turned back to the pot on the stove, hiding his need that was so painfully obvious. All he could do was give a reassuring grin over his shoulder to the inquisitive little imp.

"What did he do?" Janie asked. Leo had an answer but it couldn't be repeated in front of a seven-year-old.

"Do?" Brenda's mind still wasn't functioning. In the face of her daughter she couldn't think of a reason to hug Leo. Boy, was she in bad shape.

"I cooked dinner for a very tired, very beautiful secretary and her children," Leo inserted, finally managing to gain some semblance of control over his body. "And she gave me a hug for doing a very good job."

"But how does she know?" Janie asked. "Mommy hasn't tasted it yet."

Brenda's mind began working . . . slowly, but it was a start. "It's the thought of not having to cook that counts. Besides, I'm sure that Mr. Coulter knows how to cook spaghetti or he would have chosen something else to make." She glanced at Leo, a smile tilting her lips up beguilingly. "Right, Mr. Coulter?"

"Right," he affirmed. "This is my specialty, Janie. I only make it for special people on special occasions."

"What's the special occ—"

"That's enough," Brenda said firmly, ushering Janie out by the shoulders. "Go play until dinnertime. It won't be long."

The kitchen was silent again. Brenda turned toward Leo only to see his answering smile. "She's darling," he said softly. "They all are."

"Thanks. But they're not always so darling. Sometimes they can be downright terrible," she told him with a chuckle. "And their curiosity is never appeased."

"I bet you have a great time with them on holidays."

"Yes. It's never dull." Brenda walked over to the pantry and pulled out a package of spaghetti, opening the cellophane to begin cooking it. Leo already had the water boiling. "After David left, things were very tough. I never thought I wanted to see another holiday because it would remind me of what I lost. Instead it reminded me of what I had. Three children and a house, expensive though the upkeep might be, and a family life that he would be missing for the rest of his life." She stopped, glancing up at Leo. "I was the lucky one," she said slowly, as if she never fully realized it until that moment.

"Yes, you are." He put the spoon down and leaned against the side of the counter as he watched her add the spaghetti to the hot water. He took another deep breath as her scent wafted through the small space between them. "You don't have to worry about the holidays looming ahead and know that everyone will be with their loved ones, their families, except you. Oh, someone might invite you over out of pity, but since they're already a complete unit, you'll be an outsider. A guest."

"Is that the way you really feel?"

"Yes," he said, frowning down at the floor. He seemed almost embarrassed by the admission.

She laid her hand on his arm, giving a light squeeze. "Thanksgiving isn't that far away. Would you like to spend it with us? Not as a guest, but as a friend."

He looked at her then, his eyes filling with an emotion she wouldn't put a label to. "I'd like that very much. Very much," he repeated, his hand covering hers.

The kitchen seemed to fade away, only the strength of his arm remained to anchor her to the floor. The tiredness she had felt earlier had completely disappeared. So had her sense of despair, which seemed to follow her around. And so had much of her bitterness. She felt clean and new and sexy and very, very feminine.

This feeling was because of Leo. He accepted her as she was and for what she was, and it felt wonderful. It was something to treasure.

They ate dinner in the kitchen because Leo refused to allow her to use the dining room for such a messy meal. Besides, the kids didn't want to have to put on manners while twirling spaghetti. Leo and the children kept a fun-filled, bantering conversation going while Brenda leaned back and relaxed, watching and enjoying it. Leo would tease them and they would tease back, obviously liking him more every minute for being able to understand their special brand of humor.

After dinner the children began their homework. Only this time the girls went to the dining room table to work and left the kitchen to Leo and Brenda.

"You don't really have to help, you know," Brenda said as he pulled out plastic wrap to seal the leftover salad. "After all, you cooked."

"I know, but it's no bother." He grinned, his eyes twinkling as he watched her wiping off the tabletop, her pert little bottom gracefully moving with each wide swipe. He'd love to tell her how cute it was, but he knew the minute he opened his mouth, she'd clam up, putting that stiff reserve between them. She'd probably believe that he was making a pass to get her into bed—and she'd be right. "In fact, I like it."

She glanced over her shoulder, seeing where his eyes were glued, and blushed. Was he thinking that she was overweight? That she had too much padding when he was used to a slimmer, taller woman? Probably. Then why accept her invitation to Thanksgiving? *Because he wanted to be with a family instead of a date, stupid!* She should thank her lucky stars that he had chosen her family so she could feel the magic of the holidays, too.

She realized that at some point he would move on to another woman, probably one that suited his tastes and life-style better. But meanwhile she could enjoy him. Looking back, she owed him a lot. She had built a shell around herself and that shell hadn't been penetrated until he came along.

Now, when he left she would be able to date again, to lead a more normal life than the one she had been living. Perhaps, when he was gone, she'd go out more, at least have some adult entertainment occasionally. It would do her good.

He had done her good.

It wasn't until after the late-night news that Leo made a move to leave. The children had been in bed for hours. Leo and she had sipped what was left of the Chianti and watched TV, each in a separate chair. Leo wouldn't get close to the couch again. He eyed it as if it were half-alive and ready to inflict pain in every muscle of his body.

Finally he stood and stretched. "Time to head for home," he said, as if reluctant to put it into words. His entire evening hadn't gone at all as planned. By now he was supposed to be undressing her, one article of clothing at a time, kissing every exposed area. He quickly squelched that thought. It did too many things to his own body, and ever since they had cleaned up from dinner, Brenda had been acting reserved and distant. Apparently, when she had caught him drooling at that well-formed bottom, she had decided that she knew what he wanted and wasn't yet prepared to give it to him.

Brenda had stood when he did, watching him like a very wary cat whose tail was in his path. She wasn't too far from wrong. He grinned, unable to hide the thoughts that had been churning in his head all night long.

"Thank you for dinner. It was wonderful to come home to a cooked meal," she said shyly, not quite sure what to say or do. Suddenly she felt very awkward. Next to the chic, sophisticated, long-legged redheads he knew, she must look like an ungainly, waddling, little duck. The ugly duckling. And he was playing the part of a magician, temporarily making her feel like a swan.

Neither said a word until Leo was standing at the opened door, letting in the cool night air as he stared down at this slip of a woman. The chill came between them, making him feel as if he was using it as a ruse to leave quickly, ignoring the feelings that kept pressing to the forefront. Feelings that said take her, hold her, touch her. Kiss her.

"Oh, hell," he muttered, slamming the door with his foot as he pulled her toward him, his arms encircling her in a tight imprisoning band of muscle. His lips melded to hers, taking away her breath with his brand of possession. He was hard, demanding, silently telling her of his needs and wants.

It was as if a dam had been broken. Had Leo been gentle with her, she would have been able to keep her facade in place, but not under the onslaught of his barely leashed control. Her arms went around his neck, pulling him even closer.

A low moan escaped her throat as his tongue plunged into the soft vulnerability of her mouth, almost touching her very soul with his seeking. His hands began a tortuous journey up and down her spine, molding her shapely lines to his larger ones. She could feel his breathing as his ribs pressed into her breasts. His legs were strong, thick, corded. His need pressed into the indentation of her belly, probing, seeking her own heat.

One hand traveled under her arm and circled her breast, holding it, touching it, then teasing with fingers that trembled slightly. His very vulnerability tugged at her heart. He was as shaken by the chemistry between them as she was. Her hands stroked his neck, his shoulders, his chest, soothing the emotions that seemed to run between them, giving them both time to cool down.

His lips pulled away, foreheads touched, breathing was ragged for both of them.

"I want you, Brenda. I want you badly." His voice was raw with passion.

"Shhhh," she whispered, laying a finger across his lips. "I know."

"Will you let me take you to bed?" he persisted, unwilling to allow her ignorance of his demands. "Are you going to let me make love to you the way I want to?"

She closed her eyes tightly, warring with the two halves of herself that both wanted and didn't want the complications that Leo Coulter brought into her life. "I..." she began, not really knowing what she was going to say.

Leo sighed heavily. "You're not, are you?"

"Leo, I..." she began again.

"The answer is no. At least for now. Right?"

"Right," she said, wondering wildly if that really was the answer she was seeking.

He kissed her eyes, her cheeks, the tip of her nose. "Okay, Brenda. We'll play it your way until you can tell me out loud that you want me in your bed," he finally said. "But don't lie to yourself. You want me. You want me almost as much as I want you."

"I know," she whispered, tears forming in her eyes. A lump clogged her throat. "But I'm not a way station for some other woman's passenger."

"There is no other woman, Brenda. Just you."

Now it was her turn to sigh. "But there will be. As soon as you're tired of playing family man, you'll go back to your redheads."

"Damn you, Brenda!" he growled angrily. "I'm talking about right now, and you've already got me out the door and into someone else's arms! Can't you take it one step at a time and stop playing fortune-teller, giving both of us a future neither knows to be true yet?"

Her eyes were big and brown and so very, very sad. "But there's so much you don't know about me. How can you want to take a woman to bed when you don't know her?"

"I feel like I know you," he said quietly. "I'm asking to get to know you better."

"Oh, but—"

"What don't I know about you that you think might make me run in the other direction as soon as I find out?" he asked, his voice low and sexy, running over her body like silk.

"I have fat thighs and stretch marks," she said without thinking. Then she realized what she said and her face blazed with red.

His chuckle began as a rumble but soon turned to out-and-out laughter.

Suddenly she felt so stupid. "Stop it!" she exclaimed, pummeling his chest. "Get out of here, Leo Coulter!"

He tried to pull himself together, but the smile and the merriment in his eyes remained. "I'm sorry," he said, still restraining the laughter in his voice and trying to act solemn. It certainly wasn't the easiest job he had ever done! "But I don't care about your stretch marks. You've had three children, and I didn't think they came from cabbage patches. As for your thighs, I haven't seen any evidence of them being fat. As a matter of fact, every time I look at that darling tush of yours, all I want to do is give it a squeeze. It's tempting beyond words, believe me."

"This is crazy," she muttered, brushing her hair away from the side of her face.

His hand came up to cup her chin and lift it toward his. "Is that why you've never had an affair?" he questioned quietly.

Her brown eyes widened. "How'd you know?"

The grin came back. She had answered both questions. She had never had an affair before, and her self-image was very poor. "My God," he said, glancing to the heavens. "Thank you."

Her eyes narrowed, her lips pursed together enticingly. "You're making fun of me."

"No, sweetheart. I'm not. I'm just thankful that you've kept these misconceptions about yourself long enough for me to come along and knock them down. You're fine just the way you are. You're real and warm and loving. If you weren't those things, you wouldn't be the special person you are."

She couldn't look at him, couldn't see the humor in the situation at all. Her hands stilled on his chest.

"Brenda. Very soon I'm coming over and taking you out. After we have dinner and drinks and dancing, we're going to bed with each other. Naked. With lights on. I'll make love to you until you believe me. In return you can check out my appendix scar, circumcision and a burn scar I received as a kid when I sat down on a still-hot barbecue grill. The viewing will not necessarily be in that order." His voice deepened. "*This* is not a fortune-teller talking. This *will* happen. I'll give you a few days to deal with it and come up with whatever it takes for you to accept it as fact. This is the way it will be. Understand?"

"Why?"

"Because I'm going to go crazy if I don't take you to bed. End of explanation." How could he tell her more when he wasn't sure of it himself.

"Yes, sir," she said. "I'll think about it."

"Do that," he murmured as he kissed the tip of her nose. He couldn't kiss those lips without going through the agony of cooling down again. It was too painful to try his body's patience once more.

When he left, Brenda stood in the hallway, not moving from the spot where he had held her close to him.

He had told her he was going to climb into her bed, whether she wanted him to or not. He had told her, and she hadn't said a word against the idea. As a matter of fact, she had been in agreement! Was she out of her mind?

Well, when the time came for Mr. Leo the Lion to make his move, she'd be ready.

The answer would be no.

LEO STEPPED INTO THE COOL NIGHT AIR and almost immediately wanted to turn around and go back into the warmth of Brenda's arms. But he would have ruined that great exit. Besides, if he went back, she'd turn him away; he could see it in her eyes. She needed time, but he wasn't willing to give her much. He was in her life for an indefinite period of time so she might as well get used to it. Quick.

Whistling, he got in his car and headed for the freeway. By the time he was home, he was relaxed, tired and ready for bed. But when he was between the sheets, his mind wouldn't turn off and allow sleep to overcome him.

Every time he thought of Brenda's confession of fat thighs and stretch marks, he grinned in the dark to himself. What did she think, that he was bedding her because he thought she had a beautiful body and he could hardly contain himself before he took her flesh in lust?

The grin left his face. That had usually been his reason in the past—why should it be any different with Brenda? Why *did* he want to make love to her?

When the answer came, he didn't like it. He wanted to make love to her because he cared for her so very, very much. She wasn't like the other women he had known. She was sweet, vulnerable and resilient. It was tough raising three children single-handedly while being the only breadwinner. It would be tough for a man; it would be twice as tough for a woman. Especially for a woman who wanted to be a full-time wife and mother more than anything else. He admired her spunk, loved her sense of humor and desired her more than he had ever desired any woman.

He closed his eyes, willing himself to sleep.

Tomorrow he would begin a campaign to win her into his bed. He'd worry about the whys and wherefores later.

IT WASN'T UNTIL THE EARLY MORNING, when Brenda had put the cereal bowls in the sink and was sipping on one more cup of coffee that she remembered she hadn't checked the mail the day before. Leo had been there when she arrived home, and all thoughts of routine had slipped her mind.

With heels clicking over the hardwood floor, she went to the mailbox that hung just outside the front door. Pulling out the mail, she quickly ducked inside the house again and headed back toward the kitchen and her hot coffee. The sky was cloudless, the sun shining, and she still felt the afterglow of yesterday's surprise evening.

She flipped through the mail, mentally dismissing the bills. There were always too many to worry about. One letter, however, stood out. In a plain envelope with no advertising on it, it was addressed to her with the name that she used when entering contests: "Brenda Elizabeth Hunt."

She sat down and opened it slowly, knowing intuitively that it was something she should read, instead of throwing away as junk mail.

Scanning the letter down to the signature, she began reading it again, only this time more slowly. It took three reads before she could absorb the contents.

"I won," she whispered to the empty room. Her head came up. "I won!" she exclaimed. "Finally! I won something!" Again, she read it.

Congratulations, Brenda Elizabeth Hunt. You have just won fifth prize in our National Jingle Contest for Painter's Utilitarian Paint. Your slogan will be kept on file with us to use at a later date in our new advertising campaign.

Enclosed is a voucher for your plane tickets for two to sunny Palm Springs. You and your guest will have an all-expense-paid weekend at the exclusive Palamino Hotel. Please call this toll-free number as soon as you receive this letter and we will give you further details.

The letter went on to explain the conditions, but Brenda was too excited to read them. Later, she kept telling herself. Later. Right now she had to plan for a vacation!

By the time she had made the phone call, taken copious notes on details and driven to the office, she was floating on air. But in the back of her mind she was solving the problems of baby-sitting, the weekend to choose, the clothing she could wear—and most important of all—the person she would take as her guest.

She dropped her keys and purse on her desk and stuck her head into Sam's office.

"Hi," he said, a relaxed smile creasing his face. Again she was reminded of how wonderful marriage seemed to be for him. "Come in and tell me what's happened that put that excitement in your expression. It had better be good since you're an hour late for work. I was just going to call the police and see if you met with an accident."

"Sam, you'll never guess!" she exclaimed, ignoring his final comments as she sat down in the chair across from his desk. "I won a weekend trip for two!"

"Great! When?"

"Anytime! This weekend if I can arrange it!" Brenda said, laughing."

"Tell me about it," Sam said as he leaned back, and watched her animatedly tell her story. He didn't say a word until she was through, not even when she mentioned the fact that Leo had been at her place last night and that was the only reason she'd forgotten to check the mail. Only a raised brow showed that he had picked up that point.

"And who will your 'guest' be, now that you've won this fabulous trip?" Sam teased as she finished her excited dissertation. "Anyone I know?"

Brenda slumped in the chair, frowning. "That's just it, Sam. I'm not sure."

Sam's dark hair fell across his brow as his head snapped up. "What do you mean, you don't know?" he said, astonishment lacing his voice.

One buffed nail slipped between her lips, worrying the small teeth inside. "I just don't know."

Sam took a deep breath, then asked casually, "What about Leo Coulter? You've been seeing him, haven't you?"

"Yes, but I don't want him to think that I'm trying to tie cans on his shoes and paint 'just married' on his back."

"Then tell him so. But take him, Brenda," Sam urged. "Let yourself get to know him better."

She smiled. "You sound more like a psychologist than an attorney."

"Where Leo's concerned, I probably am," he admitted with a rueful grin. "But the two of you could use a vacation, and I don't see a damn thing wrong with going away together and getting to know each other better. Who knows, you may be fated to be lovers."

"Or forever on different sides of the fence," Brenda finished.

Sam nodded. "Maybe. But continuing this Mexican standoff won't give you the answers, either."

Now Brenda was surprised, then her eyes narrowed. "Just exactly whose friend are you, Sam Lewis?"

"Both. But before you think the worst, I'd better tell you that Leo hasn't said a word about either of you. You're the one who gave me enough clues to piece things together."

"Oh," she said softly.

"So why don't you invite him?" Sam wasn't about to let go of that thought.

"Because I'm really not his type," she said dryly, trying not to acknowledge the feeling of depression that gave her. "No one would ever take me for a long-legged redhead."

"Thank goodness for that," Sam muttered just loud enough for her to hear and grin. "But I notice that, although Leo knows what long-legged redheads look like, he's been at your place more than once."

"True," she admitted. "But I'm not sure why."

"He hasn't said?"

Brenda's face colored as she remembered his speech last night. He'd made it plain as day that he wanted her. "Well," she hedged.

"That's just what I thought." Sam leaned back again, a smug smile pasted on his face. "So ask. What have you got to lose except a good time with a great guy?"

"Right," she said with more conviction than she felt. "I'll ask him tonight."

"Right," Sam echoed. "And to make sure that you and Leo have a good time without worry, Catherine and I will take care of the children for the weekend. That way you'll know they're being watched every minute."

"You can't handle them!" Brenda exclaimed, suddenly sitting up straight.

"Yes, we can," Sam said calmly. "It will be great training. Besides, Catherine has always liked your kids. She won't mind at all. It might even take her mind off her own labor and delivery coming up. She's getting tired of waiting. So, the subject is closed. Now, get the rest of the arrangements organized. If you go this weekend, you only have a few days to get ready."

"Right, boss." Brenda snapped to attention, but the smile on her face told the story more than words could. When she reached the door, she turned around to face him. "And, Sam?" she said quietly. "Thanks. For everything."

"You're welcome," Sam said equally quietly. "You deserve much more, Brenda."

She crossed her fingers and held them up for him to see. "Let's hope," she said, not even sure what she was hoping for.

7

Leo sat back in the booth of the bar and grill. Brenda had called and asked to meet him there after work. Cautiously he had agreed. Why had he been so wary? Hadn't he been playing with the idea of calling her for the same purpose all day?

After two beers, he knew why he had responded as he had. He was afraid. With her taking the initiative, he had a feeling that she had something important to say; something like telling him not to come around anymore. He didn't want to hear that. He didn't want to hear anything that severed his still-tenuous relationship with her. It was fast becoming very important to him, and without delving into it too much, he knew that he wanted it to continue.

He saw her just as she entered the doors, then stopped to wait until her eyes adjusted to the dim light of the interior. She searched the corner, found him and smiled slowly. He could feel the warmth of that smile wrap around his body and give a squeeze. His breath came out in a whoosh, leaving him dizzy for the space of a second. Such an overwhelming feeling came over him that he found himself out of the booth and on his feet before he even realized that he had moved.

She reached him, halting just a footstep away.

"Hello," she said, her voice low, yet light and airy, playing over his skin.

"Hello, yourself." His voice sounded like sandpaper. He cleared his throat and began again. "Won't you sit down?"

She slid into the opposite side of the booth, her eyes lowered, her smile drooping slightly with trepidation, anticipating the words she was going to have to say. She stalled. "Have you waited long?" she asked, her eyes now on the empty beer mug.

"No, not long." He wouldn't admit it was his second glass.

They sat in awkward silence for a few minutes while the waitress, already primed with the order, brought Brenda's white wine and another beer for Leo.

He watched her hands circle the glass as if it were a lifeline, his own thoughts as chaotic as hers must be.

"Brenda," he began.

"Leo," she began.

They both stopped, eyes locked. For the first time that Leo could remember, he blushed.

So did she.

Dammit! What was the matter with him? His hand reached out, taking one of hers from the edge of the glass. His fingers clasped hers, warming her. He smiled apologetically. "I'm sorry. Go ahead. What were you going to say?"

Relief tinged her smile. This was the Leo she knew. Her eyes lit with mischief. "I was going to make you a proposition you couldn't refuse."

"You were? I thought I'd done that. Last night."

Her lashes drifted down to fan her cheeks. "You did. I'm just following through on it."

He grinned, suddenly relaxed. She wasn't telling him not to come around anymore. She wanted to see him, too. "Go ahead. I can't wait to hear this."

Brenda took a sip of her drink, then stared at him as if she were confronting him about something, her chin in the air. "Would you like to go away to Palm Springs with me for the weekend? All expenses paid," she said in a rush, getting it all out before she lost her courage.

His face must have shown his incredulity. She quickly squeezed his hand in reassurance. "No strings attached, Leo. Really. And I understand if you say no. Really."

"Whe—" He cleared his throat. "When?"

"This weekend. Friday afternoon." Her look was a mixture of hope and dread. He just didn't know the order. Was she hoping he would turn her down? Dreading his saying yes? Or was it the other way around? He hoped—he prayed it was the other way around. There was only one way to find out. He had to answer. Other weekend arrangements, commitments would have to be handled later. Questions would have to be asked and answered, but that could wait until later, too. This was important.

His eyes narrowed, his hand squeezed hers back. "Yes."

Her shoulders slumped with relief. A smile put highlights into her eyes again. "You're sure?"

"Yes. Yes, I'm sure," he said, then frowned. "Wait a minute. You don't expect this to be one of those platonic, let's-get-to-know-each-other weekends, do you?"

Once more her lashes drifted down to hide the expression in her eyes. "No. I know better than that."

"Then you also know that I not only intend to have access to your body, but to share your bed . . . as in all night." His voice was gruff, rougher and more demanding than he had meant it to be, but he couldn't help it. He wanted it spelled out so there would be no misunderstandings later.

"You don't have to be crude. I understand what you're saying. I wouldn't have invited you if I didn't understand the rules you outlined last night."

"And knowing those rules, you're willing to take me to Palm Springs for the weekend?" Other women in his life knew the rules. But Brenda wasn't other women. Brenda didn't know one thing about divorcées dating, let alone what the average single did or did not do. His hand tightened on hers. "You know that a weekend doesn't mean love eternal? A commitment with strings attached like a pretty present? I want to take you to bed in the worst way; I've made no bones about it, but that's all."

"No love, no commitment," she said firmly, her eyes locking with his to emphasize her words as she spoke. "I'm asking you to celebrate a weekend with me. That's all. After that, we go our own way, whichever it might be. This is just a weekend date, nothing more. I'm not ready for anything else."

He nodded, satisfied she understood his own thoughts on the matter of commitment. He wouldn't admit to a funny little feeling that niggled at him. One that seemed to deflate his ego. "Great," he muttered, letting go of her hand and reaching for his beer. It tasted flat. "What are we celebrating?"

A smile dimpled her cheeks. "My weekend vacation." She leaned forward, eagerness showing in every line of her body. "Do you remember all those proof-of-purchase wrappers in my closet?" He nodded. "Well, I also keep contest information there, and occasionally I indulge postage in them. You know, coming up with why you like something in twenty-five words or less or writing jingles. Things like that."

Again he nodded.

"Well, I won fifth place in a contest for a jingle that I wrote about paint. The prize is a weekend in Palm Springs, all expenses paid. For two."

"Hey, that's great!" he exclaimed, now understanding more than he had earlier. "For two." He chuckled ruefully. "And you invited me to share your vacation."

"Uh-huh. What did you think I was doing? Splurging all my savings to catch you in my net?" she teased, knowing that he had probably thought just that. The tension between them was gone now, replaced by a relaxed camaraderie.

"I wasn't sure," he admitted guiltily. "But your winning, well, that's terrific. Have you ever won a contest before?"

She shook her head, leaning back and sipping on her wine. It tasted light and fresh. "No, but I kept trying. I always wanted to win something. I've entered enough times, but this is the first."

His eyes twinkled. "Then we really should celebrate. How about dinner tonight?"

Regret laced her expression. "I'd love to, but I can't. I have to get home."

Leo looked down at his beer. "Right. I forgot."

"I'm sorry," she said softly, her hand covering his again.

"No problem. I just remembered, I have an appointment tonight, anyway."

Brenda drew her hand back, placing it in her lap and holding it as if it was scalded. He watched the movement, but there was nothing he could say. Damn it! He should have known better than to ask her out on a weekday evening. She was so damn proud she wouldn't even let him pay for a baby-sitter. That thought brought on another question.

"What about the kids this weekend?"

"What?" She looked up, her expression remote until his words sunk in. "Oh, Sam and Catherine are going to take care of them. He insisted."

Crow's feet crinkled delightedly. "That Sam's a pushover for kids. Especially yours."

"Why?"

"Because they're really nice kids, that's why. They're great and they're all different. Each one special in his or her own way."

Her face lit up, showing him more than anything else could, how much his comments touched her. "Thank you," she said simply.

They discussed the details, the flight time and when and where they were to meet. It was all very mundane, very uninteresting to the average eavesdropper. It was what wasn't said that was of interest. Tension floated in the air as each anticipated and wondered about their plans.

His very body position, his eyes, his words all melted around his message: *I will make love to you. I will have you just the way I've dreamed of having you.*

And her own body language responded. *I'm eager to be yours for the weekend. I know it won't last, but this will be our time together. Please don't think the worse of me for asking that you make love to me.*

Finally Leo stood and paid the bill, flipping the money on the table and, taking her arm, walked her to her car. Again the conversation covered everything except what was uppermost on their minds.

"You need to think about buying a new car," he remarked gruffly.

"Maybe I'll enter another contest and win one," she said lightly, attempting to speak around the lump in her throat. She didn't know why, but she didn't want to leave him tonight. She had an awful feeling that he was dropping her off at her car only to pick up another woman, a redhead perhaps, and spend the rest of the evening with her. And Brenda would be at home alone, dreaming of one weekend to come. A weekend to treasure the memory of his being with her, while others shared him the rest of the year.

"Good night," he said, opening her door and handing her the keys. But before she could answer, he had taken her in his arms. His lips came down, claiming, then possessing hers. His hands traveled her waist and shoulders, reaching for her neck under the softness of her hair.

She wrapped her arms around his waist, feeling the barely leashed control of his body. His tongue foraged through her mouth, his silent command for her to capitulate to him. And she did, suddenly losing the fight that seemed to make her stiff. She molded to his body, her breasts pressing against his chest, her lips cupping into his, telling him just how much she wanted him. And his body instantly responded, tautening, hardening, thrusting back at her.

"Lady, you pick the damndest places to seduce me," he muttered raggedly, holding her close to him as he struggled for breath.

"Really?" Her own voice sounded none too clear.

"Here, in a parking lot. In your kitchen doorway." He pulled away and looked down at her. "Where next?"

"In Palm Springs?" she teased, her small smile forming a delightful dimpling just below the corners of her eyes. He stared at it, entranced.

"In Palm Springs," he repeated. "Only then there won't be any more teasing. You'll come through with those silent promises that have been driving me crazy. I'll make sure of that."

She drove away, a smile still on her lips. The closer she got to home, the more the smile drooped. She had so many fears about Leo and this weekend. When would she confront them all? Not until she was forced to, she told herself, and she knew that was right. She had always run away from unpleasantness if she could. And the confrontation she was going to have with herself over Leo would definitely be unpleasant.

THEIR PLANE DEPARTED at four-thirty Friday afternoon. It was a short commuter flight, taking only an hour before they were being ushered off the plane and toward the limousine that waited for them.

They walked toward it at a brisk pace, Leo looking after all the details as if he was her husband. In fact, that's exactly what it felt like, Brenda thought, a vacation that she and her husband were having. Only Leo wasn't her husband and she was just using that thought as a way to keep the panic at bay.

He was so handsome. Women at both airports seemed to covetously eye his tawny body, hoping to catch a smile or an appreciative look from his direction. His blond hair and dark brows were a handsome contrast, but his large, muscled build was the envy of more than the women. Even a few men, paunchy and balding, looked more than just a little jealous. And why not, Brenda thought. They had probably never looked that good, even in their prime. Nor had they probably had that air of self-confidence, that invisible stamp that said, *I do. I am.*

She grinned as she watched him give the luggage claims to one of the skycaps. He also had an air that said *I am a very large steamroller. Do it my way or I'll roll over you.*

His eyes glinted. "What are you smiling about, my lovely lady?"

"You," she whispered, sweetly puckering her lips so that he longed to sip at them.

"Keep that up and we won't make it to the hotel. I'll take you in the car," he growled under his breath, his eyes riveted to her mouth.

"Promises, promises," she teased, suddenly breathless with the fact that they were here, together, and soon would be alone. All alone. Her nerves were on edge as she realized the implication for the first time. It wasn't in the future anymore. They were here. Now.

"You're damn right, promises. Remember, I'm not trying to impress anyone. I don't care whether we give the driver something to remember or not."

Her eyes dared him. "Neither do I."

Slowly, very slowly, he grinned, turning on more sunshine than she could stand. She closed her eyes and swallowed before opening them again.

"Coward," he whispered against her lips, touching her just enough to make her want to lean toward him. She wanted more and he knew it. It was in his stance, his eyes, his lips as they brushed over hers again. He was taunting her as she had taunted him.

When the skycap brought their luggage, Leo opened the car door and ushered her in, then followed. The plush interior suddenly seemed more intimate than any hotel room could be. The heavily tinted windows kept out prying eyes as well as the sun's rays. The driver placed their luggage in the trunk and closed it with a thud.

"Is everything all right, sir?" the driver asked politely as he got in the car and started the engine.

Leo's green eyes, the color of the sea, bored into hers. "It will be as soon as we reach our destination," he answered, his gaze never wavering.

His hand went to her waist, resting there as if to remind her silently what he wanted from her. She placed her hand on top of his, pressing it farther into her flesh.

Slowly he moved his hand up to stop just short of cupping her breast.

"Are you hungry?" His voice rasped like hundred-proof whisky: golden dark and warm and heady.

Suddenly she couldn't hold the panic at bay any longer. Her eyes drifted around the interior of the car, resting anywhere but on him. Thinking of everything but his intentions. His intentions had been hers, until now. Now she was just frightened to death.

"I'm starved," she said brightly, grasping at straws. "Are you?"

"Yes," he replied quietly. "My hands, my arms, my eyes and my mouth are ready for a feast."

"My, my," Brenda said shakily. "You really *are* hungry."

"For you. The anticipation is killing me," he said almost in a whisper, for her ears only. His hand squeezed lightly, almost cupping her breast. Just enough to tease the pleasure back into her so there was no room for panic.

She couldn't answer. There was nothing she could say. This was what she had wanted, wasn't it? Someone special to spend the weekend with her? Someone who wanted her as a lover, even if it was just for a little while. Someone who didn't call her mother or secretary, but woman.

They pulled up in front of the hotel and the driver opened the door to let them out. The hotel manager was there to greet them, giving them a special packet with the information they would need for the weekend. They were given their key and escorted to a beautiful suite just two stories up.

The luggage was brought in and quietly but efficiently placed in the bedroom. Within ten minutes from driving up, they were in their room and alone.

"Oh, look," Brenda exclaimed nervously. "Champagne."

Leo stood by the window that looked out toward the mountains. The desert air was hot and dry, even at this time of year. The view was simple in its awesome splendor. He turned.

"Come here," he said quietly. As quietly as when he had spoken in the car. "Remember that feast we were discussing?" She nodded her head, unable to speak. "It's a feast of the senses. My eyes want to devour you. My hands want to touch you. My arms want to hold you close." How could he tell her he was almost shaking with the need to feel the satisfaction of holding her. He had thought about nothing else.

"Can't your *feast* wait until later? We just got here." She tried to smile brightly, but her mouth wouldn't work. She was frightened to death. Reality was much more fearful than the dreams she had woven. She stood as if rooted to the cream-colored carpet. Her eyes showed the fear that had been lurking there all the time. But now it was in the open, exposed for Leo to see.

He shook his head and she saw the determination in his eyes. "No. I refuse to spend the rest of the evening walking on eggs and waiting for you to bolt and run in panic," he said slowly but evenly. "I'd rather satisfy both of us and make love to you now. Then both of us can relax."

"Wouldn't you rather, uh . . ." She couldn't think of an alternate activity. Suddenly her shoulders slumped.

"I'm scared, Leo," she whispered, her voice quaking with emotion, her brown eyes so large that he could practically fall inside them. "You've done this before. You know what to do. Tell me."

"Come here," he murmured.

And she did. She walked right into his open arms, relaxing as they gently closed around her, fencing her in.

His mouth kissed her hair, his breath soft on her temple. "Brenda, darling, you won't believe this, but I feel like it's my first time, too. I've got butterflies in my stomach, just like you," he lied. What was he thinking of? That wasn't a lie, just something he said to relax her. It was true.

She pulled back. "Do you really?"

"Yes," he said. "I need you, Brenda. Will you deny me?" He told the truth. He did need her.

Shyly, but with the firm conviction that she was doing the right thing, she took his hand and walked him to the door of the bedroom. "We have too many clothes on," she murmured, turning into his arms and beginning to work on the knot of his tie.

He slid out of his jacket, dropping it on the floor as if it was a rag. His heart was beating so hard it felt as if it were coming out of his chest. His hands clenched at her hips as he attempted to hold on to patience. He had never needed it as much as he needed it now.

"Such a lovely tie," she murmured as she dropped it to the floor. Then she began on the shirt buttons. One by one until there were no more to undo. She lifted his hand from her hips and undid one button at the cuff, then did the same with the other. But when her hand reached for his belt buckle, she hestitated, then dropped her hands to his forearms.

His smile was tight. "Is that as far as you're going?"

She stared at the hair on his chest. "I think so."

The sweep of her lashes covered her eyes so that he couldn't see what she was really thinking. "Why?"

"It's been too long since I've done anything like this," she protested huskily.

"Then I'll lead," he said decisively, moving to undo the belt to her dress. After the belt came the zipper. The cool air tingled her bare flesh and contrasted with the heat of his fingers as he guided the fastening down past her waist. With one lithe movement, the dress was off her shoulders and slithered to her waist. One small tug and it fell in a pool at her feet.

One dark brow raised in question. "No slip?"

"The dress is lined," she said by way of explanation, her fingers now playing in his amber-colored chest hair. Her hand grazed a flat male nipple and it sprung to attention. His intake of breath made her look up inquiringly. "Do you like that?"

"Yes." His voice was low and gravelly, a hoarse sound that seemed to come from deep in his throat.

Her tongue flicked out to capture the small bud. She could feel him catch his breath. While she was still brave and feeling the strength of power, she reached for his belt, unbuckling it deftly before unsnapping his pants and letting them fall to the floor.

"For someone who says she had no experience, you do that very well." His arms went around her, his fingers releasing the catch on her bra and letting it fall to the floor to join the rest of the garments.

"I've had to undo the children's jeans at least five times a day when they were little," she said breathlessly, her hand still stroking his chest while his palms captured the fullness of her breasts.

His chuckle was silent but no less there. "I wasn't speaking of the pants. I was talking about that talented little tongue of yours."

A small smile played at her lips, making her dimples appear. He watched in fascination, his hands tightening on her breasts, his thumbs flicking the centers to feel them harden.

"You like?" she teased.

"You bet," he growled, impatience lacing his every move as he swiftly picked her up and strode to the edge of the bed to toss both of them crosswise on the large mattress. His face burrowed in her neck, his tongue enjoying the flavor that was solely hers.

"Caveman," she muttered delightedly as her nerve endings responded to the touch of his hands everywhere. But he couldn't hear her. He was too busy feeling the softness of her body, the pliable way she moved, the strength of her hands as they leisurely wandered over his neck and shoulders. She was everything a man could want: soft, supple, warm and totally captivating.

His hand slipped down to the juncture of her thighs, soothing the spot that made her moan deep in her throat. "Touch me, Brenda," he said hoarsely. "Touch me like I'm touching you, darling. Please."

Her body arched toward his, her legs losing their stiffness, turning to clay. Everything seemed to be centered in her midsection, tightening to a hard, tight ball of flame. Her breath came in small gasps, his touch, his feel, his very being making her heady.

Her hand clasped him, seeking to give him the same pleasure he was so intent on giving her. A groan echoed from his throat and he moved suddenly, pressing himself above her. He stilled for a moment, his lips brushing against the pulse point at the dip in her throat. She twisted, wanting, no, craving more of him. Her whole world centered around this man above her.

He savored her movements as much as he instigated them. The more she wanted him, the more she would enjoy it. And he had promised himself that he would make their first coming together as wonderful for her as he could. His hands continued to stoke fires, his own needs almost bursting inside him.

"Leo," she whispered, unable to hold on to her thoughts.

"One more minute, darling," he promised, knowing her needs now matched his.

When he couldn't take the waiting any longer, he moved over her, using the last of his control to be gentle. But Brenda had other ideas. Her hands stroked the small of his back, then moved lower, showing him with lover's language that she needed him now. When he thrust, it pierced through her to envelop her whole mind. Once more she arched to him, only this time they moved in unison, matching as they had never matched before. No one else, her mind dimly told her. No one else had ever touched her this way. They fit perfectly, hips to hips, legs to legs, breast to chest. Lips to lips. He took her with a finesse that she would have thought impossible just an hour ago.

Tension between them built to a flash point, and Leo knew that she was his. The idea had been there all the time. She was his. He reveled in the thought even as he moved over her, his lips touching her mouth, teasing her breast, sipping on the slim neck that was thrown back in sensuous abandon. He opened his eyes and gazed down at her.

She was beautiful.

She cried out in pleasure and he thrust harder, watching every vulnerable nuance exposed on her face.

"Go, Brenda," he whispered roughly. "Let go, sweetheart."

And she did. Her arms clasped him around his middle, holding on to him as if the universe were spinning out of control. Another thrust and he was soaring with her.

Waves of unbelievable pleasure seared through her body, and she clung all the tighter.

It was several minutes later that Brenda allowed her hands to drop to the bed covers. Her eyes were closed, her breathing returning to normal. A small smile played about her lips.

"I'm too heavy for you," Leo murmured. He moved sideways, his hands drifting across her warm skin as he took his weight from her.

"I liked it," she said softly. "You felt like a great woolly blanket."

He chuckled, nuzzling her neck as if he still needed to keep in touch with her. That had never happened to her before. Usually she was immediately left alone in her bed while David got up and smoked a cigarette.

"What are you thinking?" he asked, his hand still soothing her stomach.

"Nothing."

"Liar. Tell me," he demanded.

"That I love you touching me right now.

He knew exactly what she meant. How many times had he made love to a woman only to have her jump up and take a shower, leaving him alone to come back to earth? Too many to count. "I know what you mean. I like touching you."

Brenda opened her eyes and turned her head on the pillow so she could see him. "Do you?"

His eyes showed his honesty. "Yes."

"You were right, you know," she said, even more softly. "We needed to make love before we did anything else."

"Uh-huh." He watched his hands trace patterns on her soft flesh.

"But this weekend doesn't mean that either of us is committed for life," she stated firmly.

"Nope," he agreed.

"It means we're together for the weekend. No strings attached."

"Right," he lied. If she thought he was going to give her up after this, he'd better move more subtly than he planned. This was going to be a long relationship. What kind, he didn't know yet. He'd figure that out later.

"I won't corner you into something you don't want, and you won't expect me to be something I'm not."

"Of course not," he soothed.

"Good," she murmured, her eyes closing once more, a gentle sigh echoing from her lips as she snuggled down into the bed.

Within seconds she was asleep. Within minutes he had drawn the bottom of the bedspread up to cover her. Then they both slept, relaxed in each other's arms.

8

LEO WOKE FIRST. The remainder of the day's sunshine filtered through the window, trying its best to keep the world lit for as long as it could. Shadows quickly claimed what the sun could not reach.

He turned his head and stared at the woman next to him. Brenda was asleep, the bedspread pushed aside. She was curled on her side, her head resting lightly against his upper arm so as not to cut off his circulation. He grinned at no one in particular. No one had ever been as close as she was to him now and still considered his own comfort.

Her lashes were long, dark, spiky crescents against light, peach-colored skin. Freckles sprinkled over her nose and cheekbones, making her look more like a teenager than a mother of three. Her body was supple, her legs well formed. And her hand on his chest was petite, with short, nicely tapered nails buffed to a pale pink tone.

He couldn't ever remember waking up before to find someone so different from his usual companions. Her hair didn't hold a mousse or gel that stiffened the hair into a set position while she slept. Her hands were those of a working woman, not a glamour girl, more suited to dressing wriggling children, cooking and cleaning house than to showing off diamond rings and emerald bracelets.

His glance drifted farther down, only to stop again. Her breasts were full, fuller than he was accustomed to. He remembered how wonderful it was to lay his head against the softness of them. Her waist was small, her hips trim. Had she lost weight? He wasn't sure, never having seen her naked before. But his recall of her figure the night of the musical and the reality of her now told him that he was probably right. He smiled. Why? For him? For her? He couldn't begin to figure her out.

Near the tops of her thighs were a small series of stretch marks, long faded and almost unnoticeable. He wanted to touch them, feel them, absorb them. She had probably gotten them while carrying those impish Indians. Had they hurt? Suddenly he wished he had seen her pregnant, heavy with child, a small smile on her face as she patted her swollen stomach. The thought ached with pleasantness. Brenda. Mother. He had missed a lot not knowing her sooner.

Leo, my man, you're getting fanciful in your old age, he thought. And he was right. She had been someone else's wife then, and he had been a struggling, confused young man trying to find himself. He would have probably passed her up then because he wouldn't have developed a sufficiently educated palate to discern quality when he saw it.

Her sleek body was still, like a statue. Her brown hair was pushed away from her forehead, her lips slightly parted. It was all he could do not to reach out and touch her.

She stirred, her lashes fluttering, then opening slowly to focus on his lips. "Good evening," she murmured thickly.

"Good evening. Are you hungry?" His eyes were tender, his laughter gentle.

She looked at him suspiciously. "For what?" she asked, remembering his words in the car on the way to the hotel.

"For everything. But we'll start with food."

"Good," she said, pushing herself into a sitting position, taking a deep breath and pushing the hair that tumbled around her face delightfully to the back of her shoulders.

Without even realizing he did it, his hand traced the slight indentation of her spine from her neck to the small of her back, his finger light and teasing in its caress.

She shivered, grateful for the bedspread that she hugged to her front.

"Cold?" Leo's voice was husky, his hand now stealing back up to her neck.

She glanced over her shoulder and down at him, her dark brown eyes ruefully telling the story even before she gave an explanation. "Nervous."

"Still?" His brows rose as he stared at her. He could see her cheek, her pert little nose, the winged flight of her eyebrow.

"This is really all new to you isn't it?" he asked finally, marveling in the secret delight of that thought.

"Yes, but I told you that."

"So you did," he murmured. Quickly making up his mind that action was the key to end her nervousness, he hopped from the bed and walked naked across the room to the bathroom. "Come on, lazybones. Let's shower and go down to the restaurant. You'll feel better on a full stomach." Within seconds she could hear the water running.

"Yes," she muttered to herself in answer to his last comment. "But whose full stomach will I feel better on? Yours or mine?"

It was late by the time they finally wound their way down to one of the hotel's four restaurants. Their reservations had been changed when Leo, returning from the shower, had found Brenda clad in a robe from the hotel, staring at the scenery below, a glass of champagne in her hand. He had come up behind her, his arms traveling around her waist, his chin resting on the top of her head.

"What are you looking at?" he had asked.

"A different view. I've never been here before. I've never gone somewhere different and exciting and sipped champagne in a suite and watched the sunset fall over coal-black mountains." Turning just slightly, she lifted her glass up to his lips, letting him taste a drop.

He swallowed. "And what about me? Have you fit me into your 'nevers'?"

"Oh, yes." Her eyes became solemn. "You fit right smack in the middle."

"Which is exactly where I want to be," he muttered before taking her lips in a searing kiss.

The kiss led to other things and before they knew it, an hour had passed. A delightfully wonderful hour.

Now they stood at the maître d's desk, waiting for him to appear to lead them to their table. Another couple came up behind them, and Brenda turned, curious to see what type of people came to this place. But instead of finding a couple, two women stood there, both openly surveying Leo, their eyes taking on an almost greedy, hungry look.

Brenda glanced back at Leo, who seemed to be totally oblivious to their stares. Until she saw the twinkle in his eyes as he looked down at her. He put his arm around her and leaned close.

"Oh, darling," he murmured just loud enough to carry to the two women behind him. "Was it as good for you as it was for me?"

Keeping her smile just barely under control, she answered, "Oh, yes, sweetheart."

"Even though my old war wound wouldn't allow me to fulfill your every desire?" His eyes widened in innocent question.

Was he hinting at impotence? She could hardly keep the laughter back on that comment. But she tried. Brenda nodded her head. "Even though. But you were wonderful, darling."

He patted the hand that rested on his arm. "I'm glad. Perhaps next time I'll be able to move more and you won't have to do all the work," he finished just seconds before they were asked to follow the waiter to their table.

Brenda could hardly contain her giggles as they were seated. "What injury?" she choked. "What war? And with which redhead?"

He grinned sheepishly. "Do you think we entertained them enough? I thought about going into more detail, but I didn't know if you could handle that."

The giggles finally spilled forth, a low, genuine mirth that made her all the more beautiful. "I'm glad you didn't," she said finally. "I think those women got the general idea. You're hands-off." Then her eyes lost their smile. "For this weekend, anyway."

"For any weekend." His eyes gleamed. "I have an adversity to sharks, especially when they're draped in ermine and pearls."

She tilted her head. "How do you know they were sharks? They might have been nice ladies."

"I can smell a shark a mile away. Their eyes were boring into me even before you recognized them for what they were." His hand covered hers, his thumb circling her palm. "No thanks. Their kind are rampant here. They hang around looking for fun and excitement while their husbands are off making millions."

"You've been here before?" She didn't mean to allow the disappointment to show in her voice. Of course he had probably been here before; he went anywhere there were beautiful women and a paradise playground.

"Only once and it was on business. This is my first time to relax and soak up the climate." His voice was low, soft, telling her that he truly was seeing Palm Springs through her eyes.

While they ate they spoke only occasionally, keeping the conversation light and relaxed. Leo had ordered a wine that Brenda found herself going back to more than once during the course of the dinner. By the time they were ready to leave, her head felt delightfully light, her limbs floating on air.

"There's a nightclub here. Let's go dance," he said. He couldn't very well take her back to their room and make love to her all night long. He had to be patient, treat her to the things she would remember later, things that a vacation meant to a woman who had had too few in her life. Later, his body told him. Later he'd ravish her, but right now he needed to remember that this was Brenda's time.

"That sounds lovely," she said dreamily, floating down the wide, carpeted hall with him. She hadn't been dancing in years. The only thing she would have liked to do more than dancing would be curling up in Leo's arms in the king-size bed in their suite. In fact, she could probably spend all weekend in bed with Leo and not have any regrets. Relax, she told herself. Her time would come, but right now Leo wanted to dance. Besides, every man needed a rest between activities.

The bar was dark: dark paneling, dim lighting, cozy corners and sides filled with intimate booths. Leo led her unerringly to the farthest one from the people sitting around the bar. She slid in, and then he sat beside her, his arm around her shoulders. She didn't mind the closeness at all. Her fuzzy brain told her that this was where she really wanted to be. Here or the bed upstairs.

The waitress sauntered over, took their order, winked and left.

Brenda leaned her head on his shoulder. Closing her eyes and giving a soft "Mmm," she snuggled deeper.

"Don't go to sleep now," Leo warned, a thread of laughter in his voice.

"I won't. I'm just resting my eyes."

"Wonderful," he said, disgust lacing every syllable.

One eye peeped open. "Why? What's the matter?"

"I want you to be awake. I want your company. And when we go back upstairs, I want your complete attention."

Both eyes opened, her head left the warmth of his large shoulder and he almost pressed it back in place. But believing that awake was better than asleep, he left his hand at his side.

"Complete attention? What for?" Her confusion was genuine, he surmised, looking down at her.

The waitress brought the drinks, had him sign the tab and left again.

Leo waited until she was out of earshot before he answered. "Complete attention to my skills at lovemaking, Brenda. I intend to see if I've honed them enough to please you."

Even in the dim light he could see her blushing. He loved watching it. Her lashes fluttered closed only to open and show him the warmth of her dark brown eyes.

"I don't know, Leo," she said slowly. "I'm very particular. Are you sure you've honed them enough?"

"Oh, yes," he whispered in a satin-rough voice that filtered through her whole being to bring her body alive. "I think I have." His hand stole to her lap, fingering the texture of her black dress. He worked the hem of it to her thighs. "First I'm going to kiss you until you're breathless. Then I'm going to taste other parts of you: the small sensitive area behind your ears, the hollow in your throat where I can feel your pulse beat, the curve of your breasts just above the lace of your bra." His fingers dipped between her panty-hosed thighs, soothing the skin with erotic, electric touches. "Then I'm going to move lower, taking your breast and lavishing it with attention. I want to feel your skin, seek and thoroughly explore those soft places that I only had a glimpse of earlier."

She wasn't sure anymore whether the wine was making her light-headed or his speech was. She felt everything that he said, her skin prickled as it anticipated his touch. And what his hand was doing to her wasn't helping her remain in control. "What else?" she asked breathlessly, her hand clenching as it rested high on his thigh.

"To hell with what's next," he breathed roughly. "Let's go."

He was pulling her out of the booth even before she could reach for the small handbag next to her. "What?" she teased. "No dancing?"

"You'll dance, Brenda. It'll be a perfect ballet," he promised, leading her by the hand through the darkness to the hall outside and then to the waiting elevators.

Their bodies were tense with need by the time they reached the room. Brenda was glad to see Leo's hand shaking slightly as he fumbled with the key in the lock. Why should she be the only one to feel this way?

Then they were in the room and the door was slammed behind him. He turned, stilling her hand on the light switch, taking her in his arms as he kissed her hungrily.

Then, in her honor, he choreographed the most beautiful ballet.

BRENDA STOOD in the midnight-dark room and stared out at the lights below. The hotel sat halfway up a mountainside, and the view looked out at the valley below. She could see the lights of a plane as it began its descent. More people coming for a vacation. Or did they live here, she wondered.

She glanced over her shoulder at the tawny-haired man sprawled on his stomach on the bed. He didn't look at all boyish with his hair tousled, his brows drawn tight, his darkened growth proclaiming a heavy beard. His large, muscled frame was barely covered by the stark white of the top sheet. He looked more like a resting, wild animal. Once awake he would turn into the predator again.

Her heart squeezed, then skipped a beat before continuing its regular pattern. For one weekend she had tamed the tiger. He was hers. After that, all she would have were memories of what it felt like to be a treasured, seductive, wanted, feminine woman. It wasn't much, but until this weekend she didn't know she would ever feel this way. She had Leo to thank for that. He had played the part of the ardent lover superbly.

Sunday night she would go back to being mother, secretary and lonely. But for now, she was also playing a part, seeing how a woman felt when she was seduced by someone she loved.

Loved? Where had that word come from? She couldn't love Leo. She couldn't! Brenda took a deep breath and looked out the window. The plane had already landed; its lights were gone from the sky. Slowly she felt some part of her composure returning.

No, she was just grateful to him for being a white knight and rescuing her from reality for a while. She was also grateful to him for showing her that being a woman wasn't all bad.

"Brenda." Leo's sleep-sodden voice carried softly to her. "Come back to bed, sweetheart. My arms are cold."

She turned and shed her robe, slipping under the sheet. "More than that should be cold, the way you keep kicking the sheet off."

He chuckled, his arm coming around her waist as he nuzzled her neck until his head was positioned just right. Then he placed a chaste kiss on her ear. "That's not cold, either."

"No," she whispered. "I've noticed."

His arm tightened and Brenda waited breathlessly for his next move.

But all she heard was the soft, gentle snoring of a sleeping man. She smiled, closed her eyes and joined him in sleep.

THEY HAD BREAKFAST in their room. Still in their robes, they ate cross-legged on the bed, the tray between them, bantering back and forth as if they were old friends, well tuned to each other's thoughts.

Leo challenged her to a swim in the hotel's indoor pool and he beat her on the first lap of the race. They played a water-polo game with some of the other guests, Brenda quicker to dodge and feint than Leo was.

They ate lunch on the patio, fresh fruit and chicken salad instead of the luscious Mexican food, then watched a tennis match. Leo wagered with her on the results and she lost. By late afternoon they were content to stroll up the main street of Palm Springs and peek in the gallery windows at some of the beautiful works of art. Hand in hand they wandered along, content just being together. The sun was hot, the breeze cooling, all in all it was a perfect day.

By that evening, both were ready for a quiet time in their room, but it wasn't to be. They were to dine in the hotel's most exclusive restaurant and given the best it had to offer, compliments of the paint company.

Both were dressed in their best. Brenda's hands shook as she stepped into a creamy-beige lace dress she hadn't worn in years. But its style was timeless, she hoped. It pleased her to realize that it was just a trifle loose around her hips. That jogging had paid off!

But when she sat and sipped her glass of wine in the living room of the suite while waiting for Leo to emerge from the bedroom, her mind played tricks on her, telling her that she hadn't changed at all. Oh, she had dulled the sharpness of her tongue this weekend. She'd had her hair cut professionally and it was becoming. But underneath she was still the same Brenda. She hated men, she hated the idea of marriage and how it ate away at a woman, she hated the idea of committing to someone.

So what was she doing here, waiting on a male to come through the door and give his stamp of approval on her appearance?

Just then the bedroom door opened and Leo stepped out, looking like an ad from *Gentleman's Quarterly*. His smile was soft, tender, his green eyes turning darker in appreciation. He stood in the doorway, his gaze wandering over her. "You look lovely, Brenda," he said in a hushed voice.

She basked in his warmth. "Thank you," she answered past the lump in her throat. "So do you."

His eyes crinkled endearingly in the corners. "Lovely? I've been called many things, but never that," he teased, walking toward her only to stop just short of touching her.

The lump in her throat grew larger. "No. I meant handsome."

"Thank you." His hand touched the underside of her chin in a light caress. Then his thumb stroked across her slightly parted lips, going from corner to corner and then back again.

"You'll..." She stopped and cleared her throat. "You'll get lipstick on your fingers," she said.

"Stepping into the mother role again?" he teased, but his mark hit home.

"It's part of me," she snapped as she turned her body away from his. Picking up her wineglass, she strolled across the room to the window. "I'm afraid it's not something that I shed when the children aren't around." She faced him, taking a sip of her wine for courage. "I know I'm not the kind of woman you usually spend your weekends with, but it's the real me."

His eyes narrowed as he stared at her thoughtfully. The silence hung in the air like a war banner. "Are you picking a fight with me for a specific reason, or are you frightened of me? Of spending an 'illicit' weekend with a man you suddenly think you should have known longer and better?"

She couldn't answer. She couldn't think. He had said it all. And she felt like an easily read fool. "Let's go," she muttered, setting down her wineglass and practically marching toward her small silver purse on the sofa. "If we don't hurry, we'll be late. Then you'll miss your meal."

Leo didn't move, just stood there and watched her frantic motions. "What are you saying?"

She stopped with her hand on the outer door. "I'm saying that we'd better feed you, or like a bear, you'll grumble all night." She tried to brave it through, not wanting him to see her in such a vulnerable mood. "Are you ready?"

Finally Leo moved—to the sofa—and sat down, crossing one leg over the other and draping his arm along the back. He looked as if he were getting ready for a seige. "No."

She slammed the door shut. "Look, you. If you don't like this weekend, you can leave. It's my vacation and I'm going to eat." Her stance was aggressive, her legs slightly apart as if on the bow of a ship, her hands on her hips, her small chin jutting out defiantly, her eyes shooting sparks of anger and frustration. "Are you coming or not?"

Leo continued to study her. When he finally spoke, his voice was firm. "I'm glad you realize that I could leave at any time," he said, ignoring the rest of her tirade. "Because it's true. But I don't want to. I want to be with you. That's why I'm still here." He stared at her hard for a moment. "Do you want me to be here?" he asked directly, and Brenda could tell from the silver light in his eyes that he wouldn't settle for less than an honest answer.

But she tried to hedge, anyway. "Didn't I invite you along?"

"Answer the question, Brenda. Do you still want me to be here?"

She threw her purse down on the chair, now totally out of control and unable to remember what they were fighting about in the first place. "I don't have to be on the stand, Leo! I'm not a witness to a crime!"

"Aren't you?"

"No!" Her hands shook, her knees knocked and she wanted nothing more than to sit down, but she couldn't move. She was terribly afraid.

"Isn't it a crime that we've had such a wonderful time up until now and that the rest of the weekend could be spoiled because you've decided, in the space of time that it took me go get dressed, that I'm not suitable company for you anymore?"

"That's not it at all!" she cried.

"Then what is it? Have I frightened you in some way?"

"No!"

"Have I hurt you? Insulted you by telling you how lovely you look?"

"No." Her voice lost its edge. Her hands remained clenched at her sides.

"Was it because I said I thought you were mothering me?" he questioned finally. "Because if that was it, you didn't let me finish." He stood but didn't attempt to come closer to her. "I liked your mothering, Brenda," he said softly in a deep, soothing tone. "I liked the way you thought of my getting lipstick on my fingers rather than worrying about your lipstick coming off or smearing. I like it very much. No one ever worried about lipstick on me before. Only whether or not I might have ruined their makeup just before we made a public appearance."

The stiffness went out of Brenda, her shoulders slumped and her hands unclenched. Her large brown eyes stared up into his, feeling the sincerity of his words. "Oh, Leo," she murmured with a choke and a watery smile. "Oh, Leo," and she was in his arms, burying her head in his chest, sniffling. She felt like a fool. A very lucky fool.

His lips grazed the top of her head, his warm breath ruffling her hair. "Whether you like it or not, Brenda, I'm going to treasure this weekend. It's been wonderful for me."

She lifted her head, wiping a tear from her eye. "Even though I'm not a glamorous redhead?" she teased, but her eyes showed that she needed reassurance.

He nodded. "Even though you're only a very glamorous brunette," he teased in return.

She gave a small smile. "You're good for my ego, Mr. Coulter."

"Lady, you're terrific for mine," he growled before he took her mouth in a kiss that spoke of tenderness. His arms tightened, his hands turning into vises as he held her even closer to feel each and every muscle and sinew in his body.

"And if we don't get out of here now, we won't go at all," he said gruffly. "Which will it be?"

She chuckled ruefully. "You made the reservation. I guess we'd better go."

Leo gave a heavy sigh. "All right. You win. For now." But the gleam in his eyes told her that he wanted her across his bed, not seated across the table, and that knowledge made her glow on the inside.

9

BRENDA PROMISED HERSELF that she would be on her best behavior no matter what provocation Leo might send her way. After the fiasco of a fight she had just caused in the suite, she wasn't about to step out of line in the restaurant. Above all, she wanted a three-day vacation that would warm her on lonely nights from now until her memory dimmed. And nothing, not even herself, would stand in the way.

The restaurant was more elegant than any she had ever been to. Her eyes sparkled as she studied her surroundings. The seats were all designer-upholstered wing chairs. The linen was of the finest quality, the tables' legs were hand polished pecan wood, the carpeting was so thick her beige, three-inch heels snuggled into it. But it was when the menus were handed to them that Brenda realized just how sophisticated and elite the restaurant was.

Her eyes grew round, the brown turning to gold as she surveyed the menu. "Oh, my Lord," she muttered.

"What's the matter?" Leo peered over his menu to view the odd expression on her face. His concern showed instantly. "Brenda? Are you feeling all right?"

She looked up at him blankly, then back down at the menu. "I'm just stunned," she mumbled, studying the leather folder in front of her again. "I've heard about menus like this, read about them in books, but I didn't really believe they existed in this day and age."

Leo looked at his menu again, then at Brenda, a frown creasing his forehead. "What's the matter? Did you find a bug?"

This time she couldn't help but smile. Leo must be used to things like this. "No. It's what I didn't find. There are no prices on the women's menu," she explained, the dimple on her cheek giving a quick peek.

He grinned, then leisurely glanced around. "You didn't expect that in a place like this?" His opinion was obvious. So was hers.

"No. I thought things like this went out with long dresses and smelling salts." Her smile came again. "I guess I have a lot to learn about the upper crust."

With a minimum of movement, Leo traded menus with her. "If you want to see what you're missing, try this."

He waited patiently to gauge her reaction, knowing what it would be. She'd be angry.

He was wrong. She was furious.

Her eyes flashed fire when she finally looked up. "There's no sense in these prices! No wonder they don't show the women—they'd know better than to pay for this! Thirty-five dollars for a breast of chicken, no matter what kind of mushrooms and French sauce it's smothered in, is ridiculous!"

His chuckle was soft, but it still vibrated around their table. "It depends on whether or not it's cooked at home with three charming Indians running around or sautéed by a master chef from France whose only delight in life is to make his delicacies melt in your mouth," he teased. "Besides, you're also paying for the waiters hovering around you, the upholstered chair you're lounging in and the carpeting that your unshod, dainty feet are running across now."

Her brows shot up. "How did you know I had my shoes off?"

He shrugged, but there was a twinkle in his eye. "A lucky guess."

She leaned back, a rueful expression on her face. Waving her hand gracefully to include the room, she said, "I guess you've been to plenty of these types of places before."

"A few," he admitted. "And even though I knew about them, never had my date bothered to mention the difference between the two menus before. I like it."

"Sure," she said dryly. "How to be gauche and simple in one easy lesson."

He watched her, delighting in her candor. "Didn't your husband ever take you out to dinner?"

The fun left the atmosphere. So did the warmth. "Yes. We were hamburger gourmets in every fast-food restaurant in all of Orange County."

He had put his foot in his mouth that time. Silently cursing, he tried to salvage the rest of the evening. "Surely you must have gone out alone occasionally."

"Yes. To those same places. David didn't see any reason to spend his bucks on me when he could spend it on someone else and get a bigger rate of return for his money." Her voice was filled with bitterness. "But then, you're the perennial bachelor. You don't have to worry about such things."

The waiter came to the table and stopped all conversation. They ordered quickly. By the time the waiter left, the silence between them was filled with a chilling awkwardness.

Brenda knew she should have kept her mouth shut. It wasn't his fault he didn't understand what a catastrophe her marriage was. "Look, I'm so..." she began only to look up and see the cold anger in his face.

His voice was level, but his tone couldn't be misunderstood. "I know you're bitter, Brenda, but that doesn't give you license to attack me instead of your husband. We all have something in our past that could make us bitter. That doesn't mean we allow it to."

Her back straightened. Who was he to tell her what bitterness was earned or just came with the territory? "Is that so," she said sweetly, quickly forgetting her earlier resolve. "And what could have possibly made you bitter, Mr. Coulter? Some redhead turn you down for the night?" The moment she said it, she regretted her words. Damn her for putting her foot in her mouth!

He stiffened, then leaned back in his chair and stared at her. She could feel her anger dying to be replaced with a flush of embarrassment. "I told you I was married, too. Remember? A long time ago," he said quietly. "But it didn't last. She fooled around and finally settled on one man. My best friend. It hurt, but it didn't wound me for life."

She was quiet, her eyes dropping to the empty wineglass that waited to be filled. She couldn't look at him. He was right, and that startling piece of news proved it. Once again she had let her wayward mouth run away and hurt someone else. Her self-defense mechanism was keeping her from a relationship, short or long, that would give her enjoyment.

Finally she had the courage to look up. "You're right. I'm sorry," she said simply.

His smile warmed her all the way inside. "So am I. I had no right to question you about your marriage." His hand came across the table, palm up. "Peace?" he asked softly.

She glanced from his hand to his eyes. Slowly she placed her hand in his. "Peace," she repeated, equally solemn in her pledge.

"Good. Now can we eat without another battle royal?" His tone was teasing, his hand tightening on hers.

"Only if you promise to hold your 'fightin' words' till later, counselor," she replied, equally teasing. "Say," she mused, giving her next words a lot of thought, "in our suite later this evening?"

He nodded, playing along. "I'd love to postpone the fight until then. But I think I'd better warn you in advance. I'm stronger than you are," he said, still unwilling to relinquish her hand. She slowly pulled it away, hiding her eyes from him as his words hung in the air.

She took a sip of her water, then gave a seductive smile that made Leo's stomach tighten. "I'm counting on that, Leo. I'm counting on that a lot."

Later that night, after drinks in the bar with the young assistant manager of the club who was obviously proud of his new position, and after a few publicity photos had been taken to hang in someone's office, they left for the room. By the time they reached the elevator, Brenda's nerves were taut. She had rounded on Leo twice today and had no excuse for it except her own wavering ego and a great deal of panic. None of that had anything to do with him. He was just handy to vent her spleen on. And the worst thing was that he knew it, too. Then, for some reason she would never understand, she had turned around and flirted with him outrageously all through dinner. She had never been so forward in all her life!

At the time, she loved it. It felt as if she was in control, on a power trip that was as exciting as it was dangerous.

But now, when they reached the room and were alone, she knew she couldn't do what she had teasingly promised. She was just too chicken to seduce a man, let alone a man of Leo Coulter's stature. He was the epitome of the playboy who knew all types of women. He knew more about sex than she did about cooking, for goodness' sake! Hadn't he already proven that last night?

What in heaven's name had she gotten herself into!

Leo opened the door and switched on the light. He headed directly for the coffee table that held a chilled wine and several wineglasses.

"Would you care for a glass?" he asked, his back toward her as he poured the wine.

"Yes, please," she murmured, walking toward the window. She almost had to laugh at herself. In the past two days every time she had felt nervous she had walked to this damn window as if it were a security blanket. Perhaps she should take it home with her, then when she got upset she could turn to it, as she was now, and try to feel calm again. That whimsical thought made her smile.

Leo came to her side, watching her expression in the glass, which acted like a mirror now that night had fallen. "What are you thinking?" he asked, his voice low and gravelly.

She accepted the wine he offered, took a sip and continued to stare out the window. "I was thinking that perhaps I should take this window home. I seem to stand in front of it often enough."

"Only when you're nervous," he corrected softly.

"How did you know?" She slowly turned toward him, her eyes searching his . . . Did he know her better than she knew herself?

He smiled. "It wasn't hard, Brenda. Every time you step to this window I know that I'll have to come and talk to you, get you back to the present, or you'll stand here all day."

"It's a beautiful view."

"It's becoming a nervous habit," he pointed out.

"Perhaps." Still her eyes searched his face, seeing the strength and vibrancy there as well as the more than handsome features that almost stole her breath away. He was so kind, so gentle and so very, very handsome. More than she deserved.

"Drink your wine." He tipped the glass up, knowing that she needed to unwind. All evening she had fluctuated between a flirt and a recluse, and he understood a little of her uneasiness. They had had a magical time together, but it was coming to a close. They had meshed in more ways than just the physical, but was it because of this beautiful location? Was it because they seemed to be marooned on a desert island together? And when they returned to reality, to the real, everyday, work world, would these special feelings, the total meshing of themselves be the same? He didn't know the answers any more than she did.

Brenda gulped the last of her wine, her fingers tightening on the stem of the glass. Now what, her panicked mind wondered. They had talked, drunk wine and stared at the view. She couldn't think of another thing to say or do.

Leo slipped the glass from her hand and set both their glasses on the low table behind the couch. When he turned back to her, his hands rested on her small shoulders.

His gaze touched her features one by one. "Brenda, I'm not here to seek a siren," he said honestly. "I'm not looking for a worldly wise woman who knows the ropes, either." He hesitated, thoughtful for a moment, then continued, "I'm here because I want to be with you. *You.* Not a redhead, not some sophisticated, witty debutante. Just you." He smiled, seeing the vulnerability in her eyes and wishing he could wipe it out with magic words. But he wasn't sure what she needed to hear. He only hoped that his declaration would ease her strained expression. "I liked being with you," he said simply.

He could feel the tension slowly drain from her. Her shoulder muscles eased, her hands dropping limply to her sides. "Am I so easy to read?" she whispered.

"Yes," he whispered back, afraid to break the mood. "I can see that you're frightened of me, but at the same time, I think I see a spark of desire in your big brown eyes."

"Think?"

"Hope."

"Know," she sighed, resting her head on his chest and feeling the strength of his beating heart against the softness of her cheek.

His arms encircled her and he held her close, breathing in the soft fragrance of her hair, his eyes closing in sensuous delight. She fit against his body perfectly, curving and touching in exactly the right places to make him feel strong and manly and tender and loving, all at the same time.

They stood there for a long time. But as the minutes clicked by, the safe retreat of each other's arms became tense once again, only this time the cause was an intangible need that arced between them. The need to caress, to touch . . .

Leo's arms dropped, his hand taking hers as he led her through the living room to their bedroom.

They undressed by moonlight and made love in the path of moonbeams that ribboned across the large bed. They slept contentedly cocooned in a summer-light sheet and each other's arms.

Brenda woke once in the night to find that she had worked her way to the edge of the bed. Leo lay on his side facing the other direction, his broad back a study worthy of Michelangelo. The room was warm, but she was cold. Cautiously she moved toward him, curling against him spoon fashion, her arm winding around to rest on his abdomen, her cheek against his back.

A smile curled her mouth. She felt so content, so wonderfully complacent, being near him. Her last thought was how quickly she had become accustomed to sleeping with him.

WHEN MORNING CAME into the room with a blinding intensity, Brenda hid her head under the pillow. Suddenly a soft scraping noise echoed through the room and it darkened, and she gave a weary sigh. Leo was closing the curtains they had left open last night. She turned over and went back to sleep. By the time she woke again and glanced at her watch, it was almost noon. For just a few seconds, she lost her bearings, forgetting where she was in her panic to get out of bed and start the day. Her feet hit the floor with a thud, she stood, and then, in confusion, she looked around to find something familiar.

Leo stood in the doorway, freshly showered and casually dressed in a knit shirt and shorts, a cup in his hand and a twinkle in his eyes. "Welcome to the land of the living. You're in Palm Springs."

Her eyes lit with laughter. "Do you always wake up knowing where you are?" she teased.

"Nope. That's why it's so refreshing watching someone else do what I did."

"Was it as good for you as it was for me?" she said silkily, delighted to wake up and find him waiting for her.

"You little devil," he murmured, chuckling. Bending over, he planted a kiss on her sleep-softened lips. She answered by placing her arms around his neck, giving a low moan.

"This could be habit forming," she said, smiling until she saw a look she couldn't name cross his face. "Just teasing," she added lightly as she backed away, dancing toward the bathroom. "Out in a jiffy," she called as she shut the door behind her.

"You'd better be," he growled as he walked back into the living room, a frown on his face. "The coffee won't stay warm forever!"

He practically stomped to the pot sitting on the coffee table and topped his cup. "Damn woman," he growled again. His good mood had vanished when she had admitted their kisses were a chemical explosion between them, only to renounce it the moment the kiss was over. They *were* good together! It *could* get habit forming! At least for him. Why did she have to back away from every little statement that sounded in the least like a commitment, he asked himself. Couldn't they enjoy each other without her worrying about what their relationship would be like in the future? It was always on her mind. He could tell by her comments that she was afraid of commitment, but was it because of him or just because she was afraid, period? He didn't know and was too scared to ask her.

He smiled ruefully. He could take on criminals, other attorneys, even judges. But he couldn't take on one small woman who was the most vulnerable, wonderful, sweet-and-sour person he had ever met. So much for the macho male.

By the time Brenda appeared the coffee was cold, but she made a face and drank it anyway. Leo watched her from the window she had been staring out last night. In her white shorts and peach top, she propped her feet on the coffee table and leaned back, completely relaxed. "What would you like to do today?"

"Go back to bed?" He formed the request as a question, one brow wiggling lecherously.

She giggled. "Don't believe your own publicity, Leo."

He shrugged, looking like a mischievous little hulk of a boy. "Why not? You did."

"Didn't you know? All men are supposed to be heroes in public," she said by way of explanation.

"And in private?" he prompted.

"In private they're supposed to be romantic, yearning for favors from their ladies, unguarded in their masculine way." Brenda crossed her ankles and took another sip of the cold coffee.

"Is that anything like the myth that men want women who are demure and sweet in public but tigers in bed?" His face was wiped of everything except innocence.

Brenda almost didn't swallow the coffee. "That's some demented man's wish," she explained sweetly.

"Like your explanation of males is a demented woman's wishful thinking?" he asked, his eyes narrowing as he waited for his bait to raise her temper.

Instead she nodded her head in agreement. "Exactly," she confirmed.

"And how would you like your man to be?" He hoped his tone was casual enough. He wanted an answer, but he didn't want to frighten her into retreating.

"Strong in private," she answered without a second's hesitation.

One dark brow rose in question. "Figuratively speaking, of course," she added, realizing he could take

that many ways. Her skin blushed to match the peach
tint of her cotton top.

"And in public?"

"Witty and warm."

He sat down next to her, taking the cup from her
hands and placing it on the table. "I promise that at
lunch I'll be witty and warm if you adjourn with me to
the bedroom now so I can show you just how strong I
can be in private." His look was compelling, letting her
know in no uncertain terms what he wanted from her.

She swallowed hard. Her hands began perspiring
with the need to touch the flesh beneath his shirt. Her
heart pounded in her breast. "I think that could be arranged," she finally said in a very soft voice. To her ears
it sounded like a squeak, but to Leo it was a sonata
played in heaven.

"On second thought," he murmured gruffly as he
kissed her neck and shoulder. "Why don't we make love
right here, on the floor?"

"But what if . . ." she croaked.

"No what ifs." His hand searched for the bottom of
her shirt, finally finding it and slipping his warm fingers underneath so he could stroke the softness of her
breasts. She caught her breath as his touch heated her
flesh. "The door is chained. You're completely in my
hands now, Brenda."

And within seconds, she was.

THEY SAT AT THE CANOPIED outdoor restaurant,
picking at their lunch. Their lovemaking still shone in
Brenda's eyes as she glanced up at Leo, her body still
tingling from their ardency.

"Happy?" Leo asked softly, his hand reaching out to push a stray lock of hair behind her ear.

She nodded, smiling.

"Ready for a nap?" His voice sounded so hopeful, she had to laugh. It was a delightful sound that ran through his body like warm, rippling water.

"Oh, no, Mr. Coulter. This afternoon you're taking me into town so I can buy a few T-shirts for the kids. You've been the strong, silent type all morning. Now it's time to be warm and witty."

He sighed heavily, pushing away the last half of his sandwich and opting for his foaming beer instead. "All right, Brenda, if that's the way you feel about it, but you don't know what you're missing."

"Yes, I do," she said teasingly. "Why do you suppose it was such a hard decision to make? But if I don't show up with something special for the kids, they'll remind me of my neglect for the rest of my life."

They found three perfect T-shirts. They were identical except for the colors. By the time they were finished with shopping, the sun was blazing, its heat wilting everything in sight, including them.

Siesta time was at hand, but when they finally reached their room it was time to ready for home. They carefully packed their bags, neither looking at the other as they made quick work of it.

Brenda didn't want to acknowledge that their weekend was over. But the fact thrummed in her head in rhythm to her pulse. The weekend was over. It was as if a heavy pall hung in the air. In less than four hours they would be back home, facing the thought that they would be at work in the morning. Tomorrow the children would be clamoring for breakfast, the house would need cleaning, the laundry would be piled high. All the things that comprised her slice of life would once more continue in her orbit.

And Leo would be part of her memory. A little something to treasure late at night when she was alone. Where would they go from here? Where would their relationship lead? She sighed, pushing her hair back as she bent over to slip one more item into the bag. Probably nowhere. This was a special moment out of time, but when they were back into their own separate routines, Leo would get caught up in his own social life, drifting away quickly. Oh, he would attempt to see her now and then, she knew, if for no other reason than that his own conscience wouldn't allow him to just drop her. But those times would become further and further apart, until she faded and blended into his memory along with a hundred other women before her.

As if he could read her mind, he spoke. "Brenda?"

"Yes?" She glanced up to find him at the bedroom door with his brown leather suitcase in hand. The lump in her throat grew so large she could hardly swallow.

"We're going to continue to see each other when we're back home," he stated gruffly, and she wondered who he was making that promise to, himself or her?

"Okay," she said, shrugging her shoulders before finally closing her own case.

"I mean it."

"I'd like that, Leo."

"But you don't believe it," he declared.

She shrugged again, her eyes riveted to the case on the bed. "Perhaps."

The thud of his suitcase dropping echoed through the quiet suite. In four giant steps he was in front of her, holding her tightly as if he would never let her go. "Then believe this," he muttered before his lips came down on hers, masterfully claiming the kiss as a brand. His brand.

She relented immediately, twining her arms around his neck and pulling him closer as she returned his kiss, motion for motion. Tears filled her eyes, desperation filled her heart as she clung to him, to the weekend, to the wonderful feeling of feminity that she seemed to wear whenever he was near.

He pulled back, his thumb gently touching her cheek to dry a tear. "Why?"

"I'm crying because it's been such a wonderful weekend." Her voice was husky with the lie. "Thank you."

His lips turned upward, his hazel-green eyes smiling sadly. "Thank you," he said quietly.

Then it was time to go.

10

THE PLANE RIDE HOME was just as silent as the one three days before. Only this time there was a different, more subtle tension between them. Leo felt it and knew Brenda did, too. A heavy pall of sadness tinged the air.

In less than two hours he would be dropping Brenda off at Sam's and wending his way to his own home. The weekend would be over and everything would be back to normal. Tomorrow he would walk into his office and begin the same dull routine. A case he had been working on for a while now, a mismanagement of funds between a businessman and his millionaire wife, was going to trial next week and would need all his attention. It should prove a challenge.

He glared out the window. So where was the anticipation? Why weren't the wheels squeaking that usually turned in his head, heralding the beginning of his efforts at the fight? *What the hell was the matter with him?*

The stewardess asked them if they would care for a drink. Brenda opted for Coke, but Leo ordered a small bottle of whisky and poured it in the glass, neat. He needed a little help in figuring out this new mood of his.

Brenda. He didn't want this relationship to end. He had met her under adverse circumstances and yet he'd been fascinated by her from the very beginning. First by her animosity and then by her struggle to keep a family and career together. Having raised his younger brother and put him through high school and college, he had an idea what Brenda was going through. His brother, Jason, had been fifteen, almost grown, when their parents had died, but it had still been a chore and a drain on him financially. Emotionally, it had been the toughest thing he had ever done. Jason had resented their parents for dying and he had resented Leo for trying to finish the job of raising him. Every day was a battle, every week a war won or lost on another front. By the time Jason was twenty-one, Leo had lost more than money and time. He had lost the closeness that only a family could bring. Both Jason and his wife had left him, and the only remaining memories were filled with a residue of bitter loneliness.

But Brenda was coping with three small children. They were darling, but they were still a big responsibility. His glare softened as he thought of the children. Always a pushover for kids, he had taken to hers right away. Each was so different from the other. Kingsley was at constant war with himself, trying to be both the man in the family and a young, carefree boy. Maggie was a natural mother hen, always keeping an eye on the other two in her shy way, but not knowing quite what to do when she found they were doing something wrong. And the youngest, Janie. Well, that one was going to be a real charmer. She had the makings of a siren and the quick mind of an accountant. And it was all to Brenda's credit that they didn't show many of the symptoms that other children from broken homes did. They were marvelous.

What the hell are you going to do, Coulter? Marry her? No. He shook his head. A confirmed bachelor didn't need a ready-made family to drive him nuts.

But that didn't mean he should stop seeing her. . . .

He took a gulp of his drink and continued to glare out the window at the fluffy clouds below.

Brenda's hands circled the clear plastic glass that held her soft drink. *He wishes we were home and he was by himself,* she thought sadly. She straightened in her seat, deliberately not glancing toward Leo. This was crazy. Leo was the man she had asked to go away with her so she could have a wonderful, romantic weekend and feel once more like a beautiful, desirable woman without the cares and responsibilities that usually plagued her day-to-day world. That was all. He had accepted because he couldn't see turning down a warm, willing body. The end.

Don't make more of this than there is, she warned herself. She sipped at the drink in her hands, not tasting anything. In little more than an hour she would be dropped off at Sam and Catherine's and Leo would be gone from her life, stepping back into the pages of her memory like Prince Charming in a fairy tale. And she would carry off her part in the scene with aplomb if it killed her.

"So," she said brightly, finally turning to Leo, who looked as surprised by her action as she was. "Tomorrow is a working day," she ended lamely.

"So it is," he said, once more staring out the window.

Brenda made a small face. So much for conversation. Should she try again? Why not? "Do you think it will rain tomorrow?"

His blond hair caught the sun's rays as he turned back to her, his dark brows raising in silent question to her motives. "I haven't got any idea."

"Neither do I."

A grin tugged at his mouth as he watched her stare down at her now-watery drink. "Do you care?"

"No," she said, faltering. She glanced up at him, then quickly looked down. "I just wanted to break this silence."

He waited a moment for her to continue, and when she didn't, he looked out the window again. But this time his hand reached for hers, holding it securely on his strong thigh.

She sighed and leaned back. He might not have said much, but his hand gave her the reassurance she needed to get through the next hour or so. At least he hadn't forgotten that she existed.

He continued to hold her hand, even when the plane landed and they walked toward the baggage area to await their luggage. She smiled up at him tentatively and he smiled warmly in return. Over and over her mind said that everything would be okay. They would see each other again, she knew it. Why else would he bother being so charming?

"Leo! Darling, how nice to see you!" A voice rang out and Brenda searched the crowd, her brown eyes darting here and there. She felt Leo's fingers stiffen and she pulled her hand away just as she saw a woman approach them. A long-legged redhead—she was beautiful. She wore a black two-piece suit with a striking white blouse and black-and-white straw hat. Forget beautiful, she was gorgeous.

"Hello, Dionne, what are you doing here?" Leo asked, a smile making his eyes crinkle as he took her outstretched hands in his.

"Leaving for Hawaii with some layouts for a new client," she said, smiling appreciatively at him. "What are you doing here? Leaving for Hawaii, too, I hope?"

"Afraid not. I'm just returning from a weekend trip," he told her.

Brenda moved away, pretending to be busy scanning the conveyor belt for the luggage. She didn't want to hear the conversation between Leo and that beautiful woman. She didn't want to know how close they were or hear about the friends they had in common. She didn't want to acknowledge any of it. It hurt too much.

Her luggage came by and she reached for it, only to be intercepted by a much larger, more masculine hand. "You could have stayed and let me introduce you," he murmured in her ear.

"I didn't want to intrude," she said stiffly, letting him put her luggage aside as he reached for his own.

"She was intruding. You weren't."

She almost wanted to laugh at that last comment, only she was afraid the laughter would turn to tears. How could that beautiful woman have been intruding when she had probably known Leo far longer, moved in the same circles he did, and had money that would buy her a ticket to anyplace she wanted to go? Brenda was the outsider. That woman *belonged*.

They found Leo's Cadillac and drove in silence to Sam's house, a comfortable duplex that had been built a few years ago. Sam and Catherine were in the process of building a large rambling ranch home on the side of a cliff in Malibu, but moving day was still several months away. When the door opened, the children tumbled out, each filled with questions that Brenda couldn't even hear let alone understand.

"Wait a minute," she finally cried, laughing and hugging their exuberant little bodies. "Let me get inside and I'll tell you all about it!"

"But what did you bring back for us?" Janie demanded, her expression telling the world that this wasn't the first time she had asked. She was obviously running out of patience with her deaf mother.

"Me," Brenda replied promptly with a look that would have quelled anyone but Janie.

"Is that all?" The little girl's eyes grew big as crocodile tears were born in the corner of her eyes.

Brenda sighed, knowing the tears were false and knowing, too, that she was a sucker for them. "No, I got something else, too, but you'll have to wait to find out." Through the moans, she glanced up, her eyes seeking the man who had come to mean so much to her. The man she probably wouldn't see again.

Sam was talking to Leo just inside the front door, his arm around a very pregnant, very beautiful, Catherine. Their voices were low compared to the children's, but their easygoing smiles showed Brenda, better than words, that everything had gone fairly smooth this weekend. If the children didn't mind at home, at least they minded Sam.

Catherine gave Sam's waist a hug, chuckled at something Leo said, then waddled graciously toward Brenda. "How goes it?" she said, smiling.

Brenda blushed, remembering the weekend. It had been wonderful, glorious, heart-stoppingly terrific. "It was nice," she said.

"Nice? Is that all?" Catherine prodded.

Brenda nodded, pretending she was looking at the works of art the children had shoved under her nose. Catherine had kept them busy with finger paints.

"Ohhh," Catherine groaned in frustration. "You and Leo make a wonderful pair, neither of you are overflowing with words."

Brenda looked up. "What did Leo say?"

"He said the weather was great." Catherine's voice was filled with disgust. "Honestly, all I wanted for my weekend of baby-sitting was just a little, secondhand, vicarious thrill. But neither of you will oblige!"

A chuckle rose in Brenda's throat. "Honestly, Catherine, you're getting as bad as Sam lately. You have to know everything."

"I know. It's catching. The longer I live with him, the more a habit it becomes," Catherine teased back. "The least you could do is humor me, at the most entertain me. A pregnant woman is supposed to be handled with kid gloves."

Sam must have heard that because he was suddenly standing next to them. "And I do, darling. I do tricks, dance, sing and tell great anecdotes. How much entertaining do you want?"

Leo walked up and Brenda immediately noticed the lack of air in the large room. Unconsciously her lips

parted and her small tongue darted out to wet them. Leo
watched with fascination, and Sam watched Leo watch.

"Aside from the weather and the nice time, did you
two enjoy yourselves?" Catherine persisted, remind-
ing Brenda of a toothache she once had.

"Very nice," Leo answered, his eyes still on Brenda.

"Very nice," she echoed, her mind unable to cope
with finding other words.

Sam continued to smile, while Catherine got more
frustrated by the moment.

"I have some delicious coffee cake in the oven,.
Would you like some?" she finally asked, not quite understanding what the tension was that filled the room.

"No, I've got to get the children squared away."

"No, thanks, but I'd better be going. I've got an early
day tomorrow."

Once more the air stirred with awkward tension.

It took Brenda five minutes to round up their over-
night bag and shoo the children in the car. It took her
another two minutes to say her thanks and goodbyes.
It took her the entire ride home to get herself under
control and quell the urge to cry.

She had gotten what she wanted, hadn't she? A
weekend with a wonderful, very handsome man who
made her feel like a real, warm, feminine woman who
didn't have a care in the world. She had been treated like
a queen and made love to by someone who knew the
difference between making love and having sex. "Be
thankful you had that, you ungrateful female," she
muttered under her breath, hoping the words would
scare away the tears that wanted to form and flow.

"What, Mommy?" Maggie asked as she stood between the front and back seat.

"Nothing, darling." Brenda sighed. "Sit down and fasten your seat belt.

She was back home and sliding into the routine again as if she'd never gone, never experienced the most traumatic emotion in her lifetime.

The vacation was over.

LEO SLAMMED HIS CAR DOOR and started the engine, his eyes locked on the car in front of him. Brenda had the kids belted in, at least for the moment. Then she slipped behind the wheel and, without another glance in his direction, pulled away from the curb and aimed the car toward her home. He had to think this problem with Brenda through.

His hands clenched the wheel. "Damn," he muttered under his breath, not sure if he said it out of anger, frustration or both.

They had just returned from one of the most wonderful weekends he had ever spent with a woman. They had made love as if they'd been created for each other, complimenting each move with a countermove that was perfect. It had never been that way for him before. Had it for her? Had it been so ordinary for her that he could have replaced her ex-husband and she not know it?

He slammed the car into drive and drove away from Sam's house, glad Sam and Catherine weren't at the front door watching him make an absolute fool out of himself by mooning over a woman driving away in an old gold Volvo!

Ever since he had been a teenager, he'd had girls fawning over him. In ninth grade he'd been the tallest boy in the class, a definite asset for the girls who had already begun to outgrow and out-hormone the others, and also the only one with a build that matched his height. He'd chosen and discarded as if he were a prince trying glass slippers on all the fair ladies of the land, but only as a game because he had been far more immature than his body was. At that age he had thought that girls were something you needed to have in order to brag to the other guys. But sports. That was real. His opinion of women hadn't changed much over the years, except the excuse for needing them was different.

He had only made a mistake once. When he was nineteen he had married the girl he thought was truly Cinderella. She was blond and tiny and reminded him of a frail flower who needed his big, strong protection against the hard, cruel world. It didn't last three months. She didn't need his protection any more than he needed her Southern-belle act. They were as unsuited as two people could be. She started seeing other men, he spent all his time off duty going out with the guys. Only when she had finally chosen his best friend did they realize they were all but divorced . They had parted amicably, both knowing what her parents had known all along. They were a mismatch.

He had never thought much about the relationships he'd had with women since.And there had been all kinds of women. But it wasn't until he became an attorney that he settled on a particular type: long-legged redheads who were decorative in public and willing in private. Until he had started looking for them, he'd had no idea there were so many redheads out there.

And then came petite, dark-haired Brenda, gumming up the works and sending his libido into orbit. She was all wrong for him. She was a family woman, a career girl, a woman you didn't blithely pursue life's pleasures with.

So what was he supposed to do?

He sped up the ramp to the freeway, edging his way into traffic, his driving almost on automatic.

He wanted to see her again. If he wasn't such a damn coward, he'd follow her home and spend the evening with her and the children. But the thought of getting kicked out of her private life was enough to keep him on the freeway and heading toward his home.

His stomach tightened as he remembered them sprawled on the bed last night, her hand running through the hair on his chest as they quietly talked. After a few minutes her hand had wandered, touching his stomach, his legs, everywhere but where he had wanted her to touch. She had driven him crazy and she knew it. Her big brown eyes had shown just how delighted she had been at his reaction.

And now, as he was driving down one of the world's busiest freeways, just the memory of their love was making him want her again. Only he wanted all of her. He wanted her wit, her anger, her surprising little twists of vulnerability and sweet, daring actions. He wanted the whole woman named Brenda, not just a part of her.

What the hell are you saying, Coulter? He didn't know. *Marriage?*

His hand hit the steering wheel in frustration. *"I don't know,"* he yelled to the car.

So much for thinking his problem through.

BY MONDAY MORNING Brenda was back to her usual self. The weekend with Leo seemed more like a dream than a reality. Something that she would treasure but was blurred on the edges by the fact that it hadn't really been a part of her life; it had been a moment out of time. Romantic, wonderful, sweet: but not real.

Sam smiled all day. One of those cat-ate-the-canary smiles he wore when he was so sure of the outcome. Only Brenda knew he was wrong. Sure, he had been matchmaking, but he had been doing so with the wrong two people. By now Leo was probably up to his neck in office work and his calendar was filled with events for the week with redheads of every size and shape.

Last night had been tough. Tougher than she thought it would be. The children had clamored for details of her trip, praising Leo and his sense of humor, his nice understanding ways, his ability to say the right things to them. His money.

"It was so neat the way he bought all those pizzas that time, Mom," Kingsley stated. "He must be rich, huh?".

"I don't know about that. He just bought pizzas, son, not the Empire State Building." Brenda had been busy wiping Janie's mouth, eradicating the macaroni and cheese they had eaten for dinner.

"Boy, Bubba was sure impressed!" Kingsley went on, oblivious to his mother's sarcasm. "He told the class about it, and they all want to come over and meet him the next time he's here."

"Meet him or eat pizza?" Brenda said dryly, scooting Janie off her chair and toward the bedroom so she could clean up the kitchen.

"Well—" Kingsley looked sheepish. "Either one. Besides, the guys want to see if he's really as big as Bubba said he was."

Brenda's brows rose in question. "Bubba or you?"

"Both," he answered, stuffing one more bite in his mouth before bouncing out of his chair and heading toward the living room to escape his mother's eye.

Maggie began stacking dishes, quietly working. Brenda watched her, her eyes filled with concern.

"And how about you, Maggie, mine? Do you think Leo's the greatest thing since sliced bread?" she asked in a soft teasing voice, wishing she could get a smile out of her solemn child.

Maggie's big eyes, mirrors of her own, looked up at her, and a smile worth waiting for peeped from the corners of her mouth. "I think he's very nice," she said.

Brenda wanted to hug her tight. Instead she grinned. "Really? So you've joined the fan club, too."

Maggie turned to the sink, piling the plates on one side. "Do you think you might marry him, Mommy?"

Brenda's mouth dried. Her tongue stuck to the roof of her mouth. The silverware in her hand bit into her palm. "What would make you think that, pumpkin?" she finally asked, dropping the offending forks and knives into the sink next to the dishes.

Maggie shrugged, her eyes looking everywhere but at her mother. "I don't know. Janie asked me."

"I see," Brenda said slowly, her mind churning. The children had never known her to date before. She'd never even brought a man home in the three years since their father had left. Of course they would speculate, think about having a father again.

"I don't think so, darling. We're just good friends, but we don't know each other well enough to have anyone jump to conclusions like that," she hedged. *Liar* screamed in her brain, but she decidedly ignored it.

But Maggie persisted. "He likes you, Mommy. He keeps looking at you with a smile on his face, just like Kingsley looks at Sandra in school."

"Sandra?" Brenda grasped at the name, thankful that Maggie had given her a new topic for conversation.

"He likes her. He even sits with her at lunch. Just like Mr. Coulter likes you."

"Well, Kingsley will like a lot of people before he finds one he wants to marry." Brenda laughed shakily as she began to run water for the dishes. "And so will you and so will I." She bent down and gave the top of Maggie's head a kiss. "Now, run along and do your homework. I'll finish up."

But thoughts of Leo haunted her all through the evening. Her kitchen was empty without him. Her bed was too large, the night too silent without his soft snoring. Her body ached for his touch, her mind cried for his understanding. Her heart wept for his love.

The final touch, however, was when she got around to unpacking her suitcase. In the bottom of the case, wrapped in bright paper, was a soft purple T-shirt. On the front it said "Love is" and showed a child's cuddly teddy bear.

Her eyes blurred with tears as she brought it to her cheek to feel the softness, only to be assailed with the scent of Leo's after-shave. She buried her face in the T-shirt, her heart beating rapidly at the thought of his lovemaking. Her eyes squeezed shut to deny the tears access to her cheeks.

Damn him! He had done it on purpose. He had set out to make her miss him. And he had succeeded.

She wore it to bed.

By morning, though, she had recovered some semblance of normal behavior. If Leo Coulter wanted to see her again, he could call. If not, she would never make the move toward furthering their relationship. She had found the nerve to ask him on her vacation, but her nerve had been all used up by that action. Even the thought of her new T-shirt couldn't give her enough courage to pick up the phone. For all she knew, it could have been a parting gift.

Now the rest was up to him.

Having made that decision, she felt better. For a while.

11

LEO HAD BEEN RIGHT. His latest case was going to be a challenge. His client, a millionairess in her own right, had been chiseled out of half her fortune by her husband's mismanagement of her funds. Leo wasn't certain why she had turned the money over to her husband to begin with, but he had botched the job from the beginning, if the records Leo had were any indication. Now Mrs. Henderson, sugary sweet on the outside with a will of cold steel hidden inside, wanted to get rid of her husband and recoup her losses in court.

Monday morning was so hectic that by noon he was exhausted. No sleep the night before hadn't helped. He had tossed and turned for hours. Finally dozing off, he would roll to Brenda's warmth, only to find a cold pillow where she should have been. It was stupid. How could he have gotten so used to her in only two nights? Preposterous.

He thought of the T-shirt he had bought in Palm Springs and had stuck in her luggage when she wasn't looking. It was his reminder and souvenir of their time together. He had sprinkled his after-shave on it, hoping that she would wear it and remember him. He shook his head. He should have bought one for himself and sprinkled *her* cologne on it, instead. It might have helped him sleep better.

No matter how busy he was, there were moments when Brenda's face would flash before him. He heard her deep, rippling chuckle over some incident, saw her luscious shape as she stepped from the shower, her skin glistening with silvered drops of water. Her big brown eyes looked up at him, all loving and soft and silently acceding to take him into the depths of her. She was everywhere he turned, filling the corners of his mind with her touch, her scent, her laughter.

And he hated it.

How was he supposed to get any work done? How was he supposed to play the wealthy confirmed bachelor when all he could think of was a single mother and her three little Indians? And in thinking about her, he became lonely. Lonely for her, the children, the close family atmosphere that seemed to envelop and surround them and make them a unit. A whole without him.

By nightfall he was angry with Brenda for making him feel this way. She was at home with her children to keep her company while he was alone in his town house with a Scotch as his nocturnal companion.

He reached for the phone several times but then drew his hand back. He didn't need her. He needed time. Time to put her into perspective. Time to get his life back on the track he had made for it and was content with before she stepped into his life.

By Tuesday morning he was resigned to his decision not to contact Brenda for at least a week. That way he would be able to control his response to her and see if it was just the magic of the moment that had overcome him or if it was real.

By Wednesday he was fluctuating. Perhaps he should see her now and get it over with. This waiting for his equilibrium to return itself to normal was murder on his nervous system! And all the while, the answer he wouldn't admit to lay in the back of his brain. He just couldn't acknowledge it. Not yet. But in the dark of the night, it spoke to him, telling him his true feelings concerning Brenda. He listened, he agreed. Then morning would come again and he would dismiss it.

By Thursday morning he had decided to ask out one of his favorite redheads. It would do him good. Besides, he couldn't hide in his town house all night, every night, wondering what Brenda was doing. But when he picked up the phone, his fingers went dead. His heart pumped erratically and he dropped the phone, disgusted with himself.

Fifteen minutes later he was dialing Sam's office, praying Brenda would answer. He gave a heartfelt sigh when she did, a small smile turning his lips upward as he imagined her sitting at her desk.

"Flynn-Sullivan and Lewis, attorneys. May I help you?" Brenda said.

"Hello, Brenda," Leo replied, suddenly at a loss for words.

"Leo?" Her voice sounded so soft, so sweet.

"Yes. Can you meet me after work and have dinner with me?"

"Tonight?"

"Yes."

The telephone wires sung in the void. Leo cursed himself for throwing this on her at the last minute. He should have remembered about the baby-sitting.

"I think I'd like that," she said slowly, and his breath whooshed from his chest. "I'll have to check with the baby-sitter. May I call you back?"

"No, I'll call you. Besides, I know of a baby-sitting agency that's very reputable. I'll call them and set it up."

"No, I. . ." she began.

"It's my treat. It's the least I can do. You took me to Palm Springs, remember?" His voice was light, teasing, and she couldn't resist.

"Okay, this time," she said, resigned. Then she realized that what she had said sounded as if there would automically be another time. "I mean . . ."

Leo chuckled. "I know what you mean, don't worry. I'll handle it on this end. Meanwhile, be ready when you get off work. I'll pick you up."

"But my car. . ."

"I'll take you back to your car later."

"Thank you," Brenda said, and then waited to hear his voice once more.

"You're welcome," he answered in a husky tone. "See you at five-thirty, then."

And the phone clicked.

The first smile since Sunday lit up Leo's face. A deep chuckle began in his chest and rumbled up his throat. He should have done this Monday! It felt so good! "Lady, you're in for a night on the town. Leo's side of town," he murmured, barely keeping himself from rubbing his hands together in glee.

Tonight he would see Brenda. He should have done it sooner. It was the first right thing he'd done since they had returned from Palm Springs.

Brenda slowly cradled the phone, her hands slightly shaking. He called! He finally called! She leaned back in her chair, smiling at the open pages of a magazine on a chair across the waiting room.

Ever since they had returned from Palm Springs, she had been waiting for the phone to ring. Oh, her conscious mind told her that it was probably over, but unconsciously she had been waiting. Even after three years of being alone, she never knew the evenings to drag so, as they did now. Or the time to halt in midflight, stringing out her nerves until she thought they would snap from the tension. Her nights were filled with dreams that only added to the problem, but her days were worse.

During the day she argued with herself that she could easily go back to her dull routine and pretend it wasn't dull. Leo was not for her. No man was. He'd been a wonderful escort, lover and friend for a weekend away, but that was all. It was time to settle back into her routine again. The fairy tale was over. How could it be more? A wealthy man with a demanding career needed nothing that she had. A divorcée with three children and bills that would make anyone cringe was not exactly the most romantic image in the world.

But he had called, anyway, and she would see him tonight, after all.

HE STOOD OUTSIDE the large swinging door of the office building, spotting her even before she was outside.

He stood so tall and broad and handsome in his dark suit. His blond hair was ruffled by the early-evening breeze. And his hazel-green eyes never left her. She smiled and the smile seemed to come from the tips of her toes.

"You look handsome," she said, stopping only when she was standing directly in front of him.

"You look beautiful," he murmured, his hand taking possession of her arm and guiding her into the car. "And I don't want to waste a minute of our time standing on a sidewalk and talking."

After walking around the front of the car and opening the door, he slipped into the driver's seat and faced her, his arms pulling her toward his lean body before she could protest. His kiss was warm and exciting, sending small jolts of lightning down her spine. His mouth molded hers, his tongue sending erotic messages that made her head swim with the wonder of it. Her hands found his neck, holding his head closer to her; she needed him even more than he needed her.

When he finally pulled away, Brenda moaned in protest. His breath was warm on her cheek. His thumb caressed her neck, touching as if he couldn't believe she was really there.

"I missed you," he muttered. "Too much."

She nodded. "Me, too."

"You're all I can seem to think about lately."

She nodded again. "I know the feeling," she said in a choked voice. Her heart thudded against his chest with the pain of holding back words she knew she could never say.

His hands tightened, then he let her go, grabbing the steering wheel instead. "Let's get the hell out of here," he growled, turning on the ignition and slamming the car into gear.

She watched his hands in fascination. They were so large, yet had such beautifully tapered fingers, and were strong but capable of being tender. She blushed at her memories. Those same hands holding the steering wheel had held her, touched her intimately, kept her in place so his body could take her to ecstasy.

She started when his hand reached out to grasp hers, bringing it to rest on his thigh, his palm covering hers so she couldn't take it back. Not that she would want to—she loved to feel the latent strength of him.

"Come closer," he muttered. "You're too far away."

She chuckled. "Much closer and you won't be able to drive."

"Driving isn't what I want to do, anyway." His hand moved her closer to the subject of his thoughts.

Traffic was congested as they drove up the ramp to the freeway and blended into the lines of cars. But Brenda didn't care. They could sit in traffic all night as long as Leo was with her. She smiled at the thought. In fact she'd rather sit in traffic with Leo than be in the only car on the road without him.

They drove in silence for several minutes. The plush interior of the car muffled the sound of the slow sensuous music from the tape player. Brenda leaned her head back and closed her eyes, reveling in the sense of contentment she felt.

"Brenda?"

"Hmm?"

"Did you find your new T-shirt?"

She turned her head and opened her eyes, delight shining in the brown depths. "I love it. It was the next best thing."

"To what?" He knew what she would say, but he wanted to hear it. He needed it after the agony of the past four days.

"To you," she said softly, a lovely teasing lilt in her voice.

He sighed. "Thank God. For a minute I didn't think you'd say it."

She tilted her head, pleased at his admission. "What did you think I'd say?"

"I didn't know. Your tongue can be barbed as well as sweet," he admitted as he turned the wheel and pulled off the freeway to the access road.

She glanced around for the first time. They were in a section of the city she wasn't familiar with. On one side of the street was a line of sophisticated specialty shops that only the very wealthy could afford. On the other side was one of the most beautiful set of town houses Brenda had ever seen.

They pulled into the driveway of one just as she was about to comment on them. She kept her mouth closed, afraid to hear his answer. Besides, it was obvious. Leo lived here. This was their destination.

He snapped the button on his visor and the door to the garage lifted. They drove in and the door silently lowered behind them.

"It's great on a rainy day," he said blandly, knowing her expression was bordering on mutinous. Once he got her inside, he'd chase her bad mood away. He knew just how to do it.

But when he opened the door and ushered her into the large, cathedral-ceilinged living room, her expression turned even more sour. He glanced around, making sure that he hadn't left dirty clothes or plates in sight.

"It's very nice." She trailed her hand along the back of the handsomely styled couch. Her throat was very dry, her eyes stinging. It was more than nice, it was beautiful—everything that spoke of good taste and money was there. The sofa was patterned in dark blue and peach, the cushion piping in white. It was extra long and the padding was luxuriously thick to the touch. It certainly hadn't come off any of the department-store floors that she had seen. Two large, tan, leather wing chairs framed the fireplace. A big oak chest, carved with a simple but effective pattern of curved lines, stood against the far wall. There wasn't a sign of newspapers, toys, dirty dishes, even dust. The place was spotless, just as if someone had set it up for a photo spread in one of those designer-house magazines. Even the plush, champagne carpeting didn't have one spot it.

"Care for a drink?" Leo asked, his hands spanning her waist as he stood behind her. His lips touched the top of her head and she closed her eyes.

"No, thank you," she said primly, not moving. She didn't want to lose touch with him. His house was a dream, but he was real.

He breathed in her scent. "Do you care for me?" he asked huskily.

She turned in his arms, his grasp lessening just enough to still hold her but allow her movement. Her eyes were large as she stared up at him, then brought her hand to cup his jaw, feeling the beginning of his whiskers tickling her palm. "Very much." She couldn't tell him how much. She wasn't even willing to admit it to herself yet.

"Show me, Brenda," he rasped. "Put me out of my misery." His hands tightened, holding her as if he never wanted her to leave.

Her other hand came up to rest on his chest just over his heart. She could feel the thudding and knew that she had no choice. She needed him as much as he needed her. With hands that were shaking, she began undoing his tie. Letting it hang on either side of his neck, she began on the shirt buttons, exposing more of his chest with the loosening of every one. Her fingers itched to feel the mat of curling, golden hair, and she gave in to the desire. His breathing became more shallow, quickening at her touch.

Suddenly he swung her up in his arms, holding her against him as his eyes burned into hers. "Damn it, Brenda. This wasn't what I had planned at all. I had planned on dining you, wining you, and then—" He stopped, realizing what he was about to say.

Brenda finished for him. "And then taking me to bed?" She grinned cheekily.

His expression was rueful. "Yes," he said, his voice becoming even deeper and more determined. "But we'll do it backward. I can't wait."

His stride, even with her in his arms, was long. He practically marched up the curving staircase to the landing above, which turned out to be the master bedroom. Brenda didn't even have time to glance around as he set her on her feet. His hand reached for the zipper of her dress even before she had her bearings. Within seconds they were both undressed and gazing at the other. The evening light was turning the room to a molten gold, tinting his skin with bronze highlights.

A spark flared inside her, spreading all the way through her body. Without thinking she lifted her hands and allowed them to wander down the length of his body. Seconds later her lips reached the very spots that her hands had teased. Her skin glided sensuously across his as she swayed side to side, and a groan escaped his lips. His hands cupped her buttocks, pulling her even closer to him, his breath fanning the top of her head. Her teeth nipped gently at the flesh of his shoulders, his chest.

"Brenda, don't," he murmured, but then couldn't remember what he was going to say.

"Don't what, Leo? Don't do this?" She kissed the hard tip of his nipple. "Or don't do this?" Her nails trailed to the juncture of his thighs, giving a lighter than air caress.

"Don't stop," he finally said hoarsely, almost completely out of control.

Within seconds they were on the large comforter-spread bed, Leo bending over her as his lips sought and found her erect nipples waiting for his touch. She closed her eyes and ran her hands over his body. He was so possessive, so very, very male. He was Leo. That explained it all.

When he took her it was with a barely gentle restraint, leaving no doubt as to who was in charge. When she soared it was his shoulder she clung to, his lips she sought, his body she blended with. It was like nothing she had ever known before, and that brought tears to her closed eyes. But she didn't know she was weeping until she heard the sob escape her throat.

Then Leo was kissing her again, his hands stroking her, gentling her as if she were a skittish animal. "Shh," he crooned, his hands smoothing the silken skin from hip to breasts, his lips poised just below her ear. "It's all right." His voice was like a tranquilizer to her shattered nerves.

Her lids fluttered opened as he moved his head and she stared at him through spiked lashes. "Did I hurt you, love?" he asked, his voice rasping in his throat, his eyes showing his concern.

She shook her head.

"Then what was it? Did I frighten you?"

This time she nodded, shutting her eyes for a moment before opening them again.

His eyes closed and he swallowed. When he looked at her again, there was a bleakness there. "Are you hungry?"

"Yes." Her fingers ruffled through an errant lock of hair on his forehead, combing it back only to have it curl forward again.

"Dinner's in the fridge. It'll be ready in fifteen minutes," he said as he rolled to the side and stood next to the bed. The evening sun had set and now the room was filled with shadows as it reluctantly gave way to night.

"Leo?" She lay on the comforter, smiling faintly. Her hair was tousled, her lips pouting from his kisses.

"Yes?" He reached for a pair of jeans on a hanger in his closet. He didn't look at her. He was afraid to.

"Come here," she demanded softly. "Please."

He slipped the jeans on up over his slim hips and zipped them before returning to the bed. When she looked up at him, his eyes showed a remoteness that made her shiver.

"You frightened me because I never felt that way before," she said. "I want to thank you."

A heavy sigh filled the air and he moved toward her, lifting her to the broadness of his chest. "You scared the hell out of me, woman. I thought I'd done something wrong and you wouldn't tell me."

"Can't you read females' emotions better than that after all your practice?" she teased, praying that he would tell her there weren't that many females in his life.

Instead he grinned. A glint appeared in his eye, as if he sensed her trap. "Didn't your boss ever tell you not to try and bait an attorney into an incriminating answer?" With that he left her and took the stairs, two at a time. "Get dressed, woman," he called over his shoulder. "I'll have wine waiting for you when you're ready."

She stretched lethargically, listening to the muted sounds that came from the kitchen. She glanced around, finally realizing the comforts of the room she was in. Along one side stretched a white balcony that overlooked half of the living room. Along the other was a wall of closets with mirrored doors that reflected the entire room and staircase. A partially open door directly across from the bed led to the bathroom, from what Brenda could see. The furniture was all massive, made of white oak. Again, it held the touch of a decorator with excellent taste and a knowledge of the man who lived here.

Brenda got out of bed and stood staring at the mirrored wall. The jogging she had taken up had firmed her muscles and the weight she had lost trimmed her waist and hips. Her hair still tumbled about her shoulders in disarray, making her look like a sexy woman who had just been satisfied by an obviously sexy man. She smiled. It was an apt description. That's exactly how she felt.

Then she looked at the mirror again, this time critically. Her heart dropped at her thoughts. She reached for her clothing and walked to the bathroom to freshen up. She should have known better than to look too close. She was dreaming if she honestly thought she was a sexy lady. That might have been her first response, but her second was to notice that there was not one small fingerprint on the mirror. No children toddled through this house to leave their mark. Probably no child ever would.

For just a little while she had forgotten that she was a hardworking single parent and Leo was a rich bachelor. . . .

Dinner was delicious, a crab salad and grilled steaks smothered in fresh mushrooms. The conversation was easy; they discussed the children. Brenda was forever amazed at his knowledge of the many demands they made. They also compared music and musicals and some of their favorite records and tapes.

She grilled him and savored every piece of information he gave her. It would be something to remember when he became bored and wasn't around any longer. She didn't put it into words, but the thought was there, lurking in the shadows. Leo would probably be in the arms of another woman within the next few weeks, as soon as the newness of her wore off. And when that happened, she wanted every little tidbit she could to savor for later.

Leo leaned back on the couch, his arms around her shoulders. He sipped on his brandy. "Enough questions about me. I feel worn out answering them. But what about you? What do you want for yourself?" They had gotten on the topic of ambition.

Her brow furrowed as she considered the question seriously. She had never really delved into what she wanted from life before. She'd always been too busy just staying ahead of the game. "I think . . ." She hesitated. "No," she said more definitely. "I know that what would please me most would be to become a millionaire so I could stay home and be a housewife again."

His hand rubbed her stomach slowly, more just a chance to touch than to be erotic. It was a closeness, a sincere gesture that affected Brenda more than she would admit. "You really enjoyed being a housewife? Most women I know don't think that's a career in itself." His words weren't derogatory and didn't put her on the defensive as she would normally be. He sounded as if he honestly would like to understand her thinking.

"I know," she said, tilting her head sideways so she could see him. "But I really think that to be a housewife and mother the right way is one of the most demanding full-time jobs around. I'm not talking about joining clubs and playing tennis or bridge all day. I'm talking *housewife* and everything it entails, from cooking well-balanced meals to teaching children about life and values in an entertaining way."

Leo chuckled. "April would never make it," he said.

Brenda smiled up at him, her eyes twinkled at the thought. "No, but what April does is exactly right for April. She would die doing what I would want to do, just as I would wilt doing what she does. She's perfect the way she is."

Leo kissed the tip of her nose as if silently telling her she was perfect in her way, too, and her heart swelled with love.

"And what about children?" he asked.

"Whose? Mine?"

"No. Would you have more children to add to the Indians you already have?"

She nodded, straight-faced. "At least nine. Everyone ought to have their own baseball team."

His brows rose. "Do you like basketball, too?"

"Love it."

"So do I. I wanted to be a member of the team more than anything when I was in high school."

She sat up and looked at him, surprise written all over her face. "You? I would have expected you to play football with your build!"

"You've said that before. But I'll tell you a secret," he went on, chuckling. "So did the coach. Especially when he saw me carrying my two hundred pounds around the court."

"Did you play basketball, then?"

"No. I never made the team. But I love the game, anyway."

She snuggled down toward his large frame. "Well, you should have insisted. You would have learned to be good at it if you'd been given the chance," she said, staunchly loyal.

"Thank you, Brenda, love, for your vote of confidence."

She closed her eyes and tilted her head toward his chest so she could cushion herself against him. Never in her life had she ever felt so safe, so secure. So content.

Until the phone rang.

The instant he picked it up Brenda knew it was a woman calling. Trying to veil his conversation by giving only short, terse answers, he was confirming a date for the next night.

The moonlight and wine and romance dimmed when she realized the results of the evening.

It was Thursday, he was free, he wanted a woman, and he had gotten her for the price of a supermarket steak and a baby-sitter. It still left his calendar open for the weekend. He had used her, but she had allowed herself to be used. It wasn't his fault. It was hers. Suddenly she felt sick.

As he hung up the receiver, she stood. "It's late, Leo. I think I'd better go now."

"It's only ten!"

"I have work in the morning," she said by way of explanation as she found her shoes and slid them on her feet. "But thank you for a lovely evening."

Without another word, they left, each deep in their own thoughts and much too insecure to divulge them.

12

SHE LOVED HIM with all her heart. She knew that now and was finally willing to face it. But facing it didn't mean that she would live happily ever after. That was a dream, the stuff fairy tales were made of. Reality was that she would have to promise herself never to see him again or she would be so badly hurt that she might not recover.

She paced the kitchen, her hands cupped around a steaming mug of tea. It was after two o'clock in the morning and she had been home for hours. The baby-sitter Leo had arranged for had been marvelous with the children. The house was neat, everything picked up, the children fed, bathed and in their beds. She kissed each of them in the darkness of their rooms, gazing down at them and thanking God for giving them to her. She had been blessed, and with or without Leo in her life, she would always have the children.

But the impression of Leo and his town house was still with her, showing up the differences between them as no words could. They might be as close as two people could be in bed, but once they were out of bed, the real world came crashing in. The most obvious difference was money. She didn't need him to tell her that she was in the poverty-stricken class compared to him.

She could no more afford to attend one of his parties than he could be happy spending her idea of a fun evening at home with the kids. His parties would require a wardrobe that would cost the earth to be in the passable group, just so he wouldn't feel ashamed of her. Her children would never be accepted in a world where everything was as spotless as in a designer home in a magazine. It just wouldn't work, even if they tried. Her family would suffer for it in the long run, and she couldn't go through that again.

Even if he loved her, which he didn't.

She forced the tears away, not wanting to give in to the hopeless feeling that swamped her. She would tell him that they couldn't see each other again. She would. The very next time they were face-to-face. After all, it wouldn't be fair to go into something this personal on the phone or in a letter.

With that decision delaying the action she dreaded most, she went to bed.

HE LOVED HER. He'd known it all along, but he had just ignored it. Until now.

But when he had dropped her off at her car and held her close once more, he had realized that it was tearing his heart out to let her go.

He stared into the empty fireplace, another brandy in his hand. It was two o'clock in the morning and sleep still eluded him. He felt like running or fighting or drinking himself into oblivion. He wanted to *do* something but there was nothing to do. Yes, there was. He could get in the car and drive to Brenda's and make mad passionate love to her until she finally admitted that she loved him, too. But he couldn't find the nerve; fear echoed through his body every time he thought of confronting her with his feelings. What if she didn't feel the same way? That thought couldn't bear close scrutiny.

And what about the fact that if he loved Brenda, he would also be taking on three precocious children? He delved at that thought like he would tongue a toothache. But there was no pain at all. He smiled. Who was he kidding? He thought those kids were adorable! *But you would be raising them, helping them grow, not watching as a spectator*, his conscience told him. Still there was no pain. He had no problem with a ready-made family. In fact the idea warmed him, filling a small void that had been there since he was a child and had wished for a family of his own. A real family, not just a younger brother who relied on him for money but couldn't have cared less about him.

His thoughts finally slowed down from their wild spin and he began carefully mapping out his campaign. All this week he would be tied up in court, but after that he would attack Brenda as if she was the one case he could not afford to lose. And he'd win.

His lips thinned. And tomorrow he would tell the cello player not to call him anymore. It was over. Whatever he had seen in her in the beginning was gone. She was dust next to his Brenda.

FRIDAY NIGHT WAS TORTURE for Brenda. Leo's terse conversation with the woman on the telephone the night before echoed in her brain all the next day. As the afternoon flowed into evening that same conversation tightened the muscles in her body so that she felt as if she had been fighting a ghost . . . and losing. She was surprised when she reached home and found no bruises.

After dinner she played children's trivia with the kids, each of them clamoring to answer one another's questions. They were fun to be with and share the evening with, and Brenda felt guilty even thinking of Leo and his unseen date. But she couldn't help it; it was never far from her thoughts.

By midnight she was curled on the couch in her T-shirt nightgown with a bowl of cold, half-eaten popcorn, watching an old movie. Frustration was now replaced by anger—anger with herself for feeling the need to have Leo with her and anger at Leo for making her fall in love with him.

She suddenly stood, dropping the bowl of popcorn on the table, and marched to the kitchen phone. Without giving second thoughts to the deed, she dialed Leo's number and waited, hoping against hope that he would answer. But the phone rang until the answering service picked it up. With shaking hands she quietly replaced the receiver and sat down at the kitchen table. He had obviously found someone else to while away his time with, and it was probably a redhead. She'd been prepared for this, knowing that she couldn't hold Leo for long, but she had never expected to endure this kind of heart-wrenching pain. Tears that she had held so long at bay finally fell.

There was nothing more she could do.

SATURDAY MORNING WAS CLEANING DAY. The kids all began on their chores as soon as they had eaten breakfast and finished watching their favorite early-morning cartoons. They were eager to get their respective tasks over with so they could run and play outside. Laundry was done, carpets were vacuumed, toys were put back on the shelves and bathrooms were scrubbed from one end to the other. After lunch they scampered out the door, and Brenda sat down with an extra glass of iced tea. Tea was her drink now. After three weeks of jogging and losing the weight she had always promised herself she would, she wasn't about to gain it back by chugging down the colas her children loved so much.

But even thinking about her weight didn't lessen the depression that seemed to fill her entire body. She still didn't have Leo. But her macabre sense of humor rose to the surface. What if she did have him? Wasn't she the one who said that she wouldn't get involved? And she had been right. The children didn't need another disciplinarian, and she certainly didn't need a man to tell her what to do at this stage of the game. No, she was depressed because she wanted to be, and it was going to stop now!

With a slam of her hand on the table, she stood. "Brenda, my dear, take yourself in hand and thank your lucky stars that you have control over the situation. Now forget about him and get to work on your coupons and rebates. You've let them go far too long!

On Sunday she and the children went to church, something they didn't do regularly enough to suit her. The children were the epitome of perfect and she couldn't help but smile in pride as she watched them march ahead of her down the church steps.

She was lucky, she told herself. She had the children and that should be enough for anyone.

She tried telling herself that on Monday morning, but when she reached work her mood was heavier than a lead weight. Sam smiled as he walked in, changed his mind about saying good-morning and with a curt nod, immediately closed himself up in his office. It wasn't any better at noon. The mood seemed to have caught Sam, too, for he had begun to slam around the office.

Around four that afternoon, Sam's voice came stridently through the closed door of his office. "Brenda! Come in here, please!"

She grimaced as she picked up her shorthand notebook. That was a definite command, not the usual request Sam made.

She tried for a smile, knowing that it was drooping. "Yes, Boss?"

"Sit down." He pointed to the chair in front of him and she dropped into it, dreading his next words as the moments silently ticked by and he continued to stare at her. But she really knew she was in trouble when he finally got up and went to the small bar in the corner, mixing up a half batch of his "famous" margaritas. They only came at the end of a tough day or when Sam was wanting to draw someone out. No one could stomach them, but no one had yet to get up enough nerve to tell him so, either.

She squirmed in her seat. "Sit still!" he commanded, handing her a frosty glass. He took a deep breath and began again. He never could stay angry for long. "Would you please explain to me what is going on that's knocked you for a loop?" he asked, impatience straining his voice.

Her eyes widened. "Nothing," she lied, hoping he'd drop the subject and knowing that he wouldn't

His eyes narrowed. "Don't hand me that, Brenda. I want to know what's going on and I want to know now!"

She stiffened at the tone of voice he used, then sagged in her chair. She knew he was asking because he cared. He was only yelling because he was probably as frustrated as she was.

"Sam, I . . ." she began, only to stop to swallow the lump in her throat that formed every time she thought of Leo. She took a quick sip of her drink, hoping to compose herself.

But Sam was ahead of her. He leaned forward, his brown eyes showing the depth of his concern. "It's Leo, isn't it?" he asked. "What has that bastard done to you?"

She gave a watery smile. "Nothing. He's been wonderful. It just won't work, that's all."

"Why?"

"Because we're too different, Sam. He doesn't need a ready-made family. He needs a woman who can move in the same circles he moves in, knows the ins and outs of his life-style, can help him rather than hamper him."

"Bull," Sam said succinctly before downing half his drink.

"It's true!" she exclaimed. "Besides, Leo isn't looking for a wife, he's looking for a good time. I can't be that good time for him. It just isn't me."

"It isn't Leo, either."

"Yes, it is."

Sam's eyes narrowed. "How do you know? Did he say so?"

"No, but he hasn't said anything else, either. He hasn't led me down a primrose path, Sam. I'm the one who's messed up." Her voice was as sad as her eyes.

"Do you love him?" he asked softly, and at her slow nod, he cursed under his breath. Coming around from behind his desk, he took the drink away from her, then pulled her up and cradled her in his arms, consoling her in the only way he knew how.

And the tears began. Once started, Brenda didn't think she would ever be able to stop crying. Sobs racked her body as she clung to him, her hands pulling at he suit.

"Cry, honey. It's good for you," he murmured. "It's okay."

It seemed like hours before the sobbing turned into an occasional hiccup. She pulled away, loosening her hands to smooth the wrinkled lapels of Sam's suit. She glanced at him briefly, then fixed her gaze on the buttonhole of his suit. "I'm sorry."

He grinned boyishly, belying the concern in his eyes. "I'm not. This is the first opportunity since I married to hold a good-looking woman in my arms."

"Besides Catherine?" she teased.

"Besides Catherine," he confirmed, his look softening as his wife flittered into his thoughts.

"You really love her, don't you?" It wasn't as much a question as a confirmation that the idea was a reality.

"Unbelievably. As much as you love Leo."

He was right and she knew it. "But it doesn't matter, Sam. He's out of my league."

"But how do you know? You haven't given him the chance to speak out, yet."

She closed her eyes to the tears that wanted to come again.

Sam placed his hands on her shoulders and gave a light shake. "Listen, all I'm saying is to give him a chance. Don't say no to something so important to you until you've been asked the question."

Brenda couldn't help the smile that appeared like a rainbow. Sam the Romantic. He couldn't imagine anyone not being as deliciously happy as he was. "Okay," she acquiesced.

"Good." He looked noticeably relieved. "Now go home and rest up. We're got a busy week in front of us. I just found out I have to be in court on Wednesday."

"Right, boss," she said as she saluted.

He kissed her on the cheek and pushed her out the door. "Goodbye."

IT DIDN'T TAKE BRENDA LONG to get back the in swing of things. She blocked out anything and everything that wasn't positive in attitude. There was no sense in acting like a dog in the manger over a man she wasn't going to marry. So there.

Every morning she purposely shooed any thought she had of him out the window before it had a chance to root in her brain. This was no time for her to be daydreaming. And every night she went to bed holding a pillow close to her.

As the days passed she was pretty proud of herself. She had kept her spirits up and her determination not to let Leo into her life in the forefront of her mind. But when the phone rang and she heard Leo's voice on the other end of the receiver, all her resolve disappeared.

"I miss you," he said, his deep voice vibrating through her body.

"Do you really?" she asked lightly, trying to keep her thoughts narrowed on the conversation and not on their relationship, such as it was.

"You know I do. I think you bewitched me. I can't seem to get through an hour in the day when I don't think of you."

Her hand clenched the receiver. "And what do you think about?"

"About your body lying across my bed. About your smile when you wrap your arms around me and hold me close." His voice lowered even more. He sounded tired but so very sincere. He stirred all those feelings that she had so successfully repressed. Her heart beat faster, she felt light-headed.

"That must be hard on you," she murmured, not knowing what else to say.

"It is. And when I make myself return to whatever I was doing, your lovely lips dance in front of my eyes and I remember how wonderful it was to kiss the sweetness of your mouth. It seems so real I almost want to reach out and trace your mouth with my finger, feeling the texture of your skin. I want my palms to touch the roundness of your hips, to sit in the indentation of your waist. I want to cup your breasts in my hands and tease them with my tongue."

"Leo, don't," she said, almost choking with need of him. A need that he was fueling just by talking to her.

"Brenda, I want you to want me as much as I want you. It's only fair," he groaned.

"Oh, Leo." Didn't he know that he already held her heart? But that wasn't what he wanted from her. And how was she supposed to break the spell he had woven if he could make her melt with just a telephone call. "I can't listen anymore. Please," she pleaded.

He gave a heavy sigh. "All right, darling. I really just called to see how you were, to hear your voice. I'm tied up in knots over a big case right now, but it should be settled soon. When it is, I want to see you."

She hesitated, then knew she had no choice. "All right."

"Until then, will you think of me?" His voice was low, still stroking her with imaginary fingers.

"Yes." Did she have a choice?

"Good night, darling."

"Good night, Leo."

It was the longest night she had ever spent. But her original decision still stood. She had to break it off before she broke in half herself. She loved him, but it would never work. Being his lover wasn't the answer for her, although it would work for him. It was just one of the many differences between them. Someday he would drop her for another woman. By that time it would be too late; she'd be over her head in love and never be able to pick up the pieces and begin again. Suddenly she realized that she already loved and cared for Leo far more than she ever cared for the father of her children. That thought was even more frightening than the others.

As the days passed Brenda realized that she was doing what Leo had said he was doing. Everywhere she looked she saw him. Everyone she talked to reminded her of him in some way. He was with her even as she typed letters or took dictation. By the end of the day she was cursing him. By the evening she was praying for him.

The days began in a rush and the pace never slowed down. By midmorning Brenda felt as if she had worked all day. When Sam called from the courthouse and snapped orders to carry down the brief he had left on his desk, she snapped back before finding one of the other girls in the office to take her place so she could get it to him.

The courthouse was crowded, as usual. Sam was supposed to be on the third floor in one of the small private rooms off the hall. It took her ten minutes just to locate him, hand him the brief and disappear back into the crowd that always seemed to hang around the courthouse.

As she stepped back out the large front doors, television cameras began whirring, questions were shouted and microphones held aloft in front of a small group on the bottom step.

Brenda stopped, holding her breath as she spotted the broad shoulders of the attorney who was talking. It was Leo, and his calm voice made order where chaos had been. Her heart beat rapidly in anticipation. She took the courthouse steps two at a time, anxious to see him in action. It wasn't until she paused just a few yards from his side that she noticed his companion for the first time.

She was a tall willowy redhead, handkerchief in hand and tears making bright eyes glow. "Mrs. Henderson won her suit, and Mr. Henderson will be responsible

for retrieval of the monies he used on business trans-
actions that weren't agreed upon by both parties. It was
a clear-cut case, gentlemen, as I'm sure those of you
who were in the courtroom can attest to." Leo's voice
was firm, authoritative and still very commanding.

The redhead next to him slipped her arm through his
and tilted her head toward his broad shoulder as if he
were her only rock. He glanced down, patting her hand
in response to her action, and Brenda's stomach nose-
dived to her toes.

"What will you do now, Mrs. Henderson?" a re-
porter asked.

"I'm going home to my father's ranch for a while. I
just want to have all this behind me so I can carry on
with my life," she said in a throaty voice, her eyes darting up to Leo's face as if for assurance. He nodded,
smiling, looking down at her as if she were a helpless
wilting flower and he wanted to be her strong stem.

"And what about you, Mr. Coulter? Where will you
be?" one of the cheeky reporters asked, eliciting grins
and chuckles from the rest of the crowd.

"Wherever I'm needed," he said slowly, still looking
down at the redhead.

Bile rose in Brenda's throat. Suddenly Leo was David and she was once more a third party to an affair that
refused to die. Another redhead! Anger seared through
her, practically sizzling her down to her toes. Of course!
His client, the one he had been so busy with that all the
time he could spare for her was a short, obscene phone
call. Men! She had been right from the beginning. They
were louses, every one! David had walked out the door
for one of those lovely, elusive creatures and left her to

pay the bills and shoulder major responsibilities. Leo was no better!

Oh, Leo was fascinated by her, all right. He was fascinated because she was different, but once the difference had worn off he had been true to form and continued with his old pattern. It was habit. She should have known.

She had been living in a dream world. Leo didn't need someone like her messing up his life with aspirations for being more than just another bed partner. He could choose any woman he wanted. How could she possibly compete with that? She was average in looks with three average children, an average mortgage and more than average debts. Leo's life was more than that, she had just forgotten for a while.

She didn't stop to think that just days ago she had made up her mind to call their relationship off. She couldn't. She was numb with grief, grief so deep that it took her breath away. With steps that were shaky, she practically ran to the parking lot across the street. She had to get away. She had to!

Brenda drove for hours. The office was being covered by one of the other girls. Sam was in court all day so there would be no more frantic typing or changing of schedules. And she had no energy to do more than push the gas pedal and steer the car. By five that evening she was drained. The anger was gone, as was the jealousy. The only emotion left was bitterness and that almost took too much energy for her to continue.

But she had done what she set out to do. She had cut Leo Coulter from her heart and her life.

LEO COULTER SLAMMED THE PHONE DOWN and cursed under his breath. This was his third phone call in as many days. According to the kids, Brenda had spent the weekend everywhere but home. And just now it had happened again. Kingsley said that his mother wasn't there, but Leo knew better. He had carried on a long conversation with the boy, forgetting that he was stalling, and enjoying the banter that he and Kingsley always seemed to get into. Finally Kingsley had admitted that he had homework and he would relay the message as soon as his mother came home. Where the hell could Brenda have gone? She never went out!

A cold chill shot down his spine. Or she had met someone else and was falling in love with him right this minute? Was she in another man's arms, sharing his kisses and moaning in delight from his caresses?

No! He unknotted his tie and threw it over the back of the chair. He knew her better than that. She wasn't the kind of woman who went from one man's arms to another. She was special. She was something to treasure and love, and as soon as he got hold of her he'd tell her so. He didn't know why he'd been so dense about it, but he had been attracted to her from their first date. He had fallen in love with her in Palm Springs, deeply and irrevocably. And as soon as he could get his affairs in order, he was going to ask her to marry him. That thought made him grimace. And she was going to say yes if he had to argue with her all day and night. Case closed.

THE MONDAY BEFORE THANKSGIVING Brenda curled up on the bed and, with nervous fingers, opened the letter that was addressed to her. Leo's office and address were imprinted on the upper left-hand corner. Inside was a scrawl a doctor would love, but the message was clear.

Am looking forward to Thanksgiving with you and the kids. Will be there early. Thanks, darling, for having invited me.

All my love,
Leo

Stunned, Brenda read the note again and again. She had completely forgotten about that invitation issued so long ago. Certainly he couldn't be serious and think that she still wanted him around when she wasn't even answering his phone calls! No one was that dense.

She had to withdraw that invitation somehow. Wearily, she lay back and closed her eyes. She'd worry about it later. When she was rested and ready to tackle more problems than homework assignments and grocery lists, she'd figure out whether or not she should call, write or have Sam explain that she did not want him for Thanksgiving.

But right now a compelling lethargy was taking over. She needed sleep.

Once more her life was a hectic routine. Cleaning had to be done, clothes had to be mended and grocery lists had to be made. On top of that there were cookies to bake and menus to plan for Thanksgiving.

Every day she felt just as lethargic as she had the day before. All her anger, her spirit, were gone.

And it wasn't any better by Wednesday evening. By the time she was in her car and fighting traffic to get home, she was ready to cry. No man, Leo Coulter or not, should be able to have such a debilitating effect on her! He was just a man!

When she pulled up the driveway, she was determined to pull herself together . . . again.

"Momma!" Janie exclaimed as she ran out the back door of the house and toward the car. "Guess what? We're having turkey *and* ham for Thankgiving! And mashed potatoes and sweet potatoes! And I get the turkey leg to eat all by myself!" Her little face held such excitement, her feet going up and down like small pistons.

Brenda gave her a hug as she came around the car. "We are, are we? And who decided this." She grinned, happy to be home with her family again. It had been a long day and coming home was the best part of it.

"Leo did. He bought all the groceries. We're gonna have a feast!" Maggie stood on the step of the kitchen door, her face excited as Janie's. "He's so neat, Mom. He let us help unpack the bag with all the good stuff in it, like cookies and candies and a great big pumpkin pie!"

Brenda stopped in her tracks, her eyes darting from Janie and Maggie, then back to the door. "Leo's here?"

They both nodded their heads, obviously pleased that they could announce it.

"In our home?"

They nodded again.

"What is he doing here? You were told no strangers were allowed in the house," she said sternly, but her heart wasn't in the scolding. She felt both hot and cold. Excitement and dread seemed to pour through her system at the same time, adding to the confusion of her thoughts. One part of her wanted to see him so badly, while the other was dying to tell him off.

"He just finished putting away the groceries, Mom," Maggie said, obviously upset at her reaction. "But he's not a stranger. He's *Leo* and he's nice and we like him. I thought you liked him, too."

Brenda straightened her spine and began to walk up the back steps. She kissed the top of Maggie's head as she passed. "I do, dear. Now, would you two go into the living room and watch TV? I need to talk to Leo alone for a few minutes."

She watched them trot in front of her and into the kitchen. Taking a deep breath, she slowed her steps. She wanted the children in the other room before she confronted Leo. In fact, she wished she could be in the other room with them. . . .

13

BRENDA TOOK SEVERAL DEEP BREATHS as she faced Leo. He looked so big and strong and very, very handsome. Her heart ached with the thought of losing him, but the thought of losing him later to someone else couldn't be borne at all.

He was standing at the kitchen sink, the freshly washed head of lettuce at his elbow looking incongruous. His suit jacket and designer tie had been thrown over one of the kitchen chairs, and his pristine white shirt was open at the collar to show a patch of dark blond hair on his chest. His shoulders were outlined by the smooth-fitting material. He was magnificent. He stood cautiously waiting.

"You aren't supposed to be here."

"But I am," he said slowly.

"Why?"

"Because I bought the groceries for Thanksgiving. And because I wanted to see you again. You wouldn't answer my calls, you wouldn't respond to my note. What else could I do?"

"Take the hint and leave me alone?" she asked, wishing she could make her words sound sweetly sarcastic, yet knowing that they came out as an emotion-filled croak.

"No." His tone was emphatic, yet sad, as if he, too, wished for that but knew the impossible couldn't be done.

"Then, if you can't take the hint, I'll spell it out for you," she said, her heart breaking as she studied his face, his stance, his very presence. "I don't want to see you again, Leo Coulter. Your type doesn't need my type. We aren't compatible."

"I thought we were," he said, still not moving from where he was.

She wished with all her heart that he would come toward her, say something that would force her to change her mind. She wished he would overwhelm her with logic and reasoning that would keep them together. Always.

But he didn't. He just stood there and stared sadly at her.

"I want you to leave and I don't want to ever see you again. I want you out of my life, my house, my children's life. Do you understand?" Her eyes flooded with tears but she refused to let them fall so they remained, shimmering in her eyes and magnifying the hurt inside.

His mouth only formed one word, but it was her undoing. "Why?"

Suddenly her nerves felt as if they were being pulled by invisible strings. She walked around the table, putting even more space between them. "Because you aren't good for us," she cried. "You and your money and your little fun things to do that will spoil the kids because I can't continue doing it. You and your kind aren't meant to enter my world and change us so that we can't operate without you. It isn't fair! I don't want you disrupting our lives like this, coming and going when it's convenient for you, as if we could slip into a closet, like a used toy, until you want to play with us the next time!" Her hands clenched the back of the chair, her knuckles turning white with the effort.

Leo shook his head, his eyes filled with sadness. "You don't mean that," he began, but she interrupted him.

"Oh, yes, I do!" she answered bitterly. "I want you out of here, out of my life! Now! Go find some red-head who can fit neatly into your life-style! Someone rich and beautiful and very, very sophisticated! Like that woman you just defended! She's just your type. You don't need a mother of three who doesn't give a damn about the parties and hoopla you're involved in. Get out of here and leave me and mine alone!"

Her words seemed to echo around the room, bouncing off the wall and finally leaving a silence that couldn't be filled.

Slowly Leo reached for his suit jacket. After shrugging into it, he walked to the door, then turned, staring down at her with eyes that seemed to touch and envelop her.

"Goodbye, Brenda," he said, and left.

The room was empty.

Brenda was empty.

And still the tears refused to fall. It was late before she got the children fed and off to bed. They bombarded her with questions about Leo, and she fended them off as well as she could. Somehow the actions of cooking, cleaning up and talking to the children seemed to be automatic. Her mind was numb, set in the cold storage of her body.

It wasn't until she fixed herself a cup of tea, cradled the cup for warmth and sat at the kitchen table that she allowed even one small thought of Leo to enter her mind. And it opened the floodgates of a thousand thoughts and scents and touches that she had remembered so vividly. She was swamped with so many emotions that she almost drowned in them. Her eyes stared straight ahead as she remembered it all in glowing detail and realized that Leo was so much more to her than any other adult she had ever known.

He was everything.

And because she was afraid to tell him how she felt, she had lost him. Her private fears had stood in the way of her own happiness. She had gotten her wish; she could now live out the rest of her life alone, without all the dreams that she had dreamed and the things that she had thought of doing. No more children, no man to talk to in the middle of the night cuddled deep in the bedding, holding hands, saying without words everything that was stored in hearts once broken and now mended.

No, that wasn't right. She might have wished aloud for peace and quiet alone, but silently, like a child crying under the covers so no one could hear, she had prayed for something quite different.

She had prayed for a man like Leo to come into her life and love her as she wanted and needed to be loved. She had wanted it so very badly, and when it had come in the form of Leo, she had turned her back on him.

A sob took her breath away.

She had made the wrong decision. She would love Leo all the days of her life. Until Leo had entered her small world, life had passed her by. God had given her another chance, and she had muffed it, going for the dross instead of the gold. Instead of treasuring the memories they had made together, she should have treasured the man.

Stupid! Stupid! Stupid! Her hand clenched into a fist and she hit the surface of the table with each exclamation. Finally her head lowered to rest on the cool surface of the table while the tears ran unheeded down her cheeks.

LEO DROVE THROUGH THE DARKNESS. He didn't know where he was—he didn't care. Driving was simply something he did when he needed to think.

He glanced at his watch, surprised and yet not surprised that he had been driving for over two hours already. The first hour had been filled with pain. The agony of her words had almost ripped him apart as he stood there like a dead man and let them eat into his flesh.

Then had come the anger. That bitch! She had led him on, made him fall in love with her and then dropped him as if he was nothing! He groaned, running a hand over his face. And still her treatment of him changed nothing. He loved her.

Why? He had never been into masochism before. What would make him continue to love a woman who hated him? But she didn't, a small voice inside him said. She loved him. The moment the thought jumped into his head he knew he was right, with a certainty that hadn't been present throughout this whole romance. She loved him and was as frightened of that emotion as he had been. Her fear was based on a man who had walked out on her, leaving her not only to raise the children by herself but to lead a life of loneliness and heartache that had taken years to recover from. She was afraid of a repeat performance.

His fear was based on taking on a complete family and doing the best job he could. What if he didn't do everything right? After more thought, though, he knew that helping her to raise the children was what he wanted to do more than anything in the world. Those kids were darling, and he couldn't imagine anything more wonderful than to help Brenda raise them to be the well-adjusted adults they showed such potential for. So what if he occasionally made a mistake? Didn't every parent?

His thoughts began to sort themselves out. Brenda was worried about going through the hell of her first marriage again, relying on someone only to have them leave her alone to face picking up the pieces. She was more than worried: she was scared to death.

Suddenly he smiled. Everything slipped into place and he finally understood. With understanding came action. He turned the car around and headed toward the nearest expressway.

Brenda didn't know it, but she was waiting for him.

BRENDA OPENED THE REFRIGERATOR DOOR, for the first time looking, really looking, to see what Leo had bought. Just like the pantry, every shelf was crammed with goodies. Fresh cranberries, fruit, celery and tomatoes were jumbled into the vegetable bin along with fresh cauliflower and her favorite, fresh brussel sprouts. Tears filled her eyes. He had remembered a late-night conversation in Palm Springs when she had admitted that she loved them.

On the large bottom shelf was a turkey. Not the sale kind but the one that promised the best flavor and was the easiest to cook. Sitting beside it was a large ham that cost more than she spent on a week's groceries.

Her sob turned into a gulp and the gulp turned into a watery chuckle. She could imagine him winding up and down the aisle of a grocery store, stopping over items and debating whether she would like them. But it wasn't the groceries that she loved him for buying. It was the fact that he had actually gone grocery shopping for her and the family. No one had ever shared that burden with her. Oh, a neighbor might have picked something up occasionally, but they hadn't really shopped. Not really. But Leo had. He had done it for her and the children, putting thought into each item he had bought, just as she did.

She reached for the ham and hugged it to her breast, staring down at it as if it was a symbol of all she had been foolish enough to lose. Her sniffles began again and she bent her head, allowing the deep well of tears to continue to fall, getting caught in the mesh string that held the ham.

When the back door slammed, she jerked, pivoting quickly to face whoever was there.

Leo stood etched against the kitchen doorway, gray against the white of the wall. His face was lined with weariness just as hers was lined with pain. But his eyes…oh, his eyes were so warm she could feel the heat from across the room.

"Tell me one thing," he said in a deep rasping voice that acted like a saw on her nerves, snapping them to threads.

She nodded, clutching the ham to her breast as if it were a plate of armor. She sniffed, then wiped the back of her hand over her wet cheeks. Incredible hope and terrible fear glowed in her eyes.

"Do you love that damn ham better than you love me?" he asked, taking one step closer to her. "Because if you do, that's all right. I'll just eat the thing and be rid of it. But I can't walk out of here again and be rid of the love I have for you. I'll settle for second best."

The ham was dropped to the kitchen table to fend for itself as Brenda practically ran into his arms. They closed around her, hugging her so tightly she couldn't breath, but she didn't care. Leo buried his face in the dark fall of hair, breathing the scent of her. His hands touched her shoulders, back, waist and hips, as if to verify she was really in his arms, where she belonged. His heart felt all in one piece again, only now it was big enough to engulf her, too. He sighed deeply. He felt full. For the first time in his life he was part of someone, and he knew this was what he had always wanted.

"I love you so much," she whispered against his chest. "I love you and I didn't want to."

"I know," he soothed, his hand touching her hair with a shaking he couldn't hide.

"I've been a fool." She hiccuped, burrowing deeper into his strong chest.

"I know," he said, a lump forming in his throat. He was holding her. She was his. His.

"I wanted you, but I was frightened. I thought you'd run off with a redhead when you tired of me."

"I know." His voice rumbled in his chest. "But you should have known better."

"I did. I didn't want to admit it." Her hands circled around his neck.

"If I had wanted a redhead, I could have had one at any time. But I didn't. I wanted you. So bad that I still hurt from your rejection."

She looked up at him, all the love in her spilling over to show in her eyes. "I know," she said, her hand running the length of his jaw. He turned his head and kissed her palm, his tongue sending darts of warmth through her body.

"You're marrying me, Brenda. No excuses. No hesitations."

"I know," she whispered, a small smile peeking out to delight him with her dimple.

"And the children will get used to me. I know they will. We'll be a family."

"I know," she said, once more before standing on tiptoe and reaching for his mouth. Her lips brushed his, then came back and brushed again, teasing, tantalizing him with promises that were made to keep. "I think they love you already."

"Oh, darling. I'm so thankful I met you," he murmured before capturing her soft lips with his. And she couldn't help the smile. They both knew.

IN THE SMALL BEDROOM decorated in pink and white, Maggie stared out the window at the moon above. "Thank you, God," she whispered. Sitting on the sill was a large pink piggy bank. Her hand closed over the top and gave a squeeze. At one time it had held three dollars and sixteen cents, but all of it had gone to the poor box in church in return for a favor.

A father like Leo hadn't been too much to ask for after all.

No one Can Resist . . .

HARLEQUIN
REGENCY ROMANCES

Regency romances take you back to a time when
men fought for their ladies' honor and passions—a
time when heroines had to choose between love and
duty . . . with love always the winner!

Enjoy these three authentic novels of love and
romance set in one of the most colorful periods of
England's history.

Lady Alicia's Secret by Rachel Cosgrove Payes

She had to keep her true identity hidden—at least until
she was convinced of his love!

Deception So Agreeable by Mary Butler

She reacted with outrage to his false proposal of
marriage, then nearly regretted her decision.

The Country Gentleman by Dinah Dean

She refused to believe the rumors about him—
certainly until they could be confirmed or denied!

Everyone Loves . . .

HARLEQUIN GOTHIC ROMANCES

A young woman lured to an isolated estate far from help and civilization . . . a man, lonely, tortured by a centuries' old commitment . . . and a sinister force threatening them both and their newfound love . . . Read these three superb novels of romance and suspense . . . as timeless as love and as filled with the unexpected as tomorrow!

Return To Shadow Creek by Helen B. Hicks

She returned to the place of her birth—only to discover a sinister plot lurking in wait for her. . . .

Shadows Over Briarcliff by Marilyn Ross

Her visit vividly brought back the unhappy past—and with it an unknown evil presence. . . .

The Blue House by Dolores Holliday

She had no control over the evil forces that were driving her to the brink of madness. . . .
